THE BURIED TRUTH

THE BURNING TRUTH

SUKKRITI NATH

Notion Press

Old No. 38, New No. 6
McNichols Road, Chetpet
Chennai - 600 031

First Published by Notion Press 2017
Copyright © Sukkriti Nath 2017
All Rights Reserved.

ISBN 978-1-948032-18-6

This book has been published with all reasonable efforts taken to make the material error-free after the consent of the author. No part of this book shall be used, reproduced in any manner whatsoever without written permission from the author, except in the case of brief quotations embodied in critical articles and reviews.

The Author of this book is solely responsible and liable for its content including but not limited to the views, representations, descriptions, statements, information, opinions and references ["Content"]. The Content of this book shall not constitute or be construed or deemed to reflect the opinion or expression of the Publisher or Editor. Neither the Publisher nor Editor endorse or approve the Content of this book or guarantee the reliability, accuracy or completeness of the Content published herein and do not make any representations or warranties of any kind, express or implied, including but not limited to the implied warranties of merchantability, fitness for a particular purpose. The Publisher and Editor shall not be liable whatsoever for any errors, omissions, whether such errors or omissions result from negligence, accident, or any other cause or claims for loss or damages of any kind, including without limitation, indirect or consequential loss or damage arising out of use, inability to use, or about the reliability, accuracy or sufficiency of the information contained in this book.

Dedicated to my baba,

Prof. Surendra Nath

A man who endlessly fought with all his courage and determination against a disease with no cure – Cancer.

You are truly an inspiration.

CONTENTS

About the Author.. xi
Acknowledgements.................................... xiii

Section 1: The Ascent 1
1. The Beginning...................................... 3
2. The (in) Significant Poem Competition 8
3. The Pre-Date Distractions 12
4. The Date... 16
5. May 13th, 2017.................................... 19
6. Best. Day. Ever.................................... 22
7. Kilig 26
8. Wolf in a Sheep's Skin 29
9. The "Good" News 34
10. Flushed down the Toilet 38
11. The Game at Avenues 42
12. The Lies 47
13. The New (Uni)Form 50
14. ~~First~~ Worst Day................................. 56
15. The Fire Drill? 63
16. Natzi Is Back 67
17. The (Un) Willing Volunteer...................... 70
18. -Truth-... 73

19. The Note 78
20. The Race I Aced. 83
21. First Day at Swimming 87
22. Swimming and Smoking. 91
23. The Revelation. 96
24. The Competition! 101
25. The Chase Begins 107
26. The Practice TEST!. 111
27. Ria's Wretched Reality 116
28. Longest Car Ride Ever. 119
29. Goosebumps. 124
30. Papa's Unusual Side 130
31. Wrong Decisions 134
32. Flip, Turn and Run! 138
33. The Irresistible Invite. 142
34. Change in Plans 147
35. Get, Set and Wait 152
36. Sharmaji vs. Sharmaji Ki Beti 155
37. Ashamed of Me?. 161
38. Insignia? 167
39. The VIP Access 172
40. The Turning (.) 176
41. The Kick (Down). 180

Section 2 : The Descent 185

42. Flashbacks 187
43. Grounded?. 191
44. Apology Accepted?. 195

45.	-Cravings-	199
46.	My New Friends :)	205
47.	The Last Cigarette	208
48.	Smoking and Bonding	214
49.	'Hiding & Smoking'	219
50.	The Dreadful Health Checkup	223
51.	When Reality Strikes	228
52.	4 Days Left	231
53.	3 Days Left	238
54.	2 Days Left	243
55.	A Day Left	246
56.	The Day of Districts: At Home	250
57.	The Day of Districts: The Beginning	255
58.	The Day of Districts: Confession #1	260
59.	The Day of Districts: Confession #2	265
60.	The Day of Districts: Heat 1	269
61.	The Post-Break up – Break Up	277
62.	The Day of the Districts: Confession #3	281
63.	The Day of Districts: Confession #4	285
64.	The Day of Districts: Final Verdict	289
65.	The Last Turning Point the Day of Districts: Heat 2	293

Epilogue 297

ABOUT THE AUTHOR

Sukkriti Nath is a fifteen-year-old first-time author, she is passionate about reading and writing and comes from a family of academicians whose roots belong to the ancient holy city of Varanasi. She lives with her parents, brother and grandmother in Gurgaon, Delhi NCR, India.

She is in her MYP – 5, IB at Pathways School, Gurgaon.

Sukkriti has written this novel to highlight the causes and impacts of teenage smoking and has depicted the same through fictional writing. She also researched the subject extensively through surveys, expert interviews and secondary sources prior to the writing.

She further intends to donate all sales revenue generated from this novel to Cuddles Foundation, which is an institution supporting child cancer treatment.

ACKNOWLEDGEMENTS

As a first-time author while writing my novel itself was courageous, writing the acknowledgments is even more excruciating. There have been so many people who have encouraged me, motivated me, helped me overcome the fear, clarified my doubts and discussed and debated – I worry how do I bring all of them in few pages.

I am deeply indebted to all of them but I would have not been able to complete this without the support of my papa – Mr. Shachindra Nath, who helped me with this book from scratch, till its present state; and my mumma – Dr. Shruti Nath who diligently edited each word of this book, several times. Without you both, I wonder who would have handled my tantrums and yet supported my decisions, and gave me all the love and guidance that I needed to complete this book.

I cannot forget to thank my brother Arush Nath, who was my pillar of strength and support throughout this journey. I would also take this opportunity to thank my entire family – dadi, nanas, nanis, mamas, mamis, uncles, aunts as well as cousins for their unwavering love and undaunted support. The best critics for my ideas were my friends, and so I wish to deeply thank them for their support whenever I needed it.

Acknowledgements

I'm immensely grateful to my mentor – Ms. Deepshikha Dhawan Sapra who critically evaluated my work and acted as the guiding light even on the darkest nights, helping me sail through the entire journey. I also wish to thank my school, Pathways School Gurgaon and all my teachers and facilitators for their continuous motivation and assistance.

I would take this opportunity to also thank my publishers – Notion Press, as well as Ms. Sona and Mr. Naveen who personally helped and guided me throughout the post-writing process of the book.

However, my journey is not over yet, I have written this book to support a cause – that would not get completed without the support of all those would promote this, purchase this and help me to raise the money for my cause of improving the life of those young ones those who are suffering from Cancer – so all those unknow to me, A big Thank You.

Section 1

THE ASCENT

1

THE BEGINNING

The referee blew a long, defining whistle. All the swimmers, dressed in tight-fitted nylon costumes, stepped on to their blocks. I could see that Aman was scared. His face clearly showed that he was nervous, since he had started to do his usual – rubbing his ears like a dog. So, I began cheering for him and in no time, all FPS girls were cheering 'East or West Aman is the best!' He looked at me and passed me his wavering smile, and then he went back to being as focused as anyone could be.

Aman is the reason why I am, who I am. I mean, before I became friends with him, things weren't the same. Earlier, I was a weird new girl, who had no clue why she was at Florens Public School, and was just desperately trying to fit in. And then, he came along – his dark-brown eyes, went perfectly with his hair. He smiled crookedly with his imperfectly thin lips. Aman was good at just about every sport, swimming being his forte and he was basically the dream boy. Plus, he already knew how to drive, and he even smoked every once in a while.

It made him seem so mature, and grown, unlike the other boys in our class, perhaps that's what had swoon me over, the first time had our eyes met.

Suddenly, the referee blew another long whistle and Aman grabbed the block handle. The entire swimming arena seemed silent. I could hear Ria breathing heavily in my ear. I could even hear my heart beat strongly and the thumping beat in my wrist.

"Stop it breathing like a camel!" I told her.

She looked at me as if I was crazy, "God, Sana! Focus on the race; it's about to start."

Ria was a sixteen-year-old girl with curly hair and dark brown eyes. Her face's most notable characteristic was her peculiarly sharp nose. But most importantly, most guys maintained their distance from her due to her excessively great height which perhaps made those boys feel insecure. Nevertheless, I considered her to be my best friend. And that's all that mattered.

My thoughts were disturbed by the starter shouting "Take your mark!" followed by a loud horn. With eyes fixated on Aman, I saw him as he splashed into the pool, making his way forward. Each of us cheered and clapped as the swimmers swam as fast as they could. It was at that moment that I felt like just jumping into the pool and swimming with them. I too, wanted to feel the cold water against my skin. I too, wanted to feel the adrenaline rush before the race begins. I too, wanted to be gleeful on winning the race.

Afterwards, we went to our school's grand dining hall. This dining hall was used for many more purposes apart from eating. It was the place where all the gangsters of the school fought with a live audience that hooted for them. The tables were used by budding romantics as a cover for 'under the table' stuff. The teachers used it as a place to judge children. But even after all of this, it was my favorite place in the 36 acre sprawling campus. I liked the dining hall because I got to always sit right in the center of the long table, a spot from where I could see everyone, that's why I hated when anyone sat on my spot.

"Hey! New girl, don't you know that Sana sits here?" Renuka, one of my minions, asked sarcastically.

I nudged Reunka, telling her to calm down.

"I'm sorry, I didn't know we have fixed seats here." She replied hesitantly.

"Well, Sana does. So, get the hell up," said Divya, my other minion.

The girl looked very scared. She was rapidly blinking her eyes, and wrinkles took over her forehead. She quickly put her glass into her tray and fled away. I vividly smiled at her, as I saw her leave, while we went for grabbing lunch.

❁ ❁ ❁

The bell rang, and we hurriedly entered the dim class, with dull walls. Our class boards were bare, and the only colorful thing present was the whiteboard markers' ink. We all sat in our usual spots. I sat down with Ria, while Aman and his friend Rohan, sat in front of us. Our teacher, Gauri ma'am, wasn't in yet.

The Burning Truth

I quickly took out a rough page, and we started playing a game that most people would call ridiculous. It was the game where the four of us, graded a person out of 10, by judging them based on brains and beauty. We had come to an obvious decision that I was a 10, and Aman was a 9. Rohan and Ria were 8s. We were debating whether Megha, the geek, was a 3 or a 2, when Gauri ma'am finally walked in.

"Good morning class," she said in her stern tone.

We all replied in chorus, "Good morning ma'am!"

Gauri ma'am was a decent teacher, but was commonly known as the Hitler of our school, and a rumor went that she once ended up punching a wall so hard, that it literally fell apart in pieces. Ever since, she is probably regarded as the scariest teacher by most students. Although I felt that if you were nice to her, she would be good to you. But she rarely displayed any emotions or feelings.

After a while, I noticed that everyone around me had gradually zoned out as ma'am talked about Macbeth and Shakespeare. But I stayed focused, I had realized recently, that I am developing some interest in English as a language.

❀ ❀ ❀

When the bell rang, Gauri Ma'am called out my name, "Sana Sharma! Please stay back, I have to talk to you."

I'll be honest, when she took my name, I almost had a minor stroke. I had a very good reputation with all teachers, but Gauri ma'am...I just didn't know. I immediately started thinking of all possible reasons why she'd ask me to stay back.

Had she found out about how I took revenge from Megha by telling my minions to chop off her hair?

Or had she realized that it was my gang who stole all the mobiles from the teacher's drawer?

Or worst, some rival of mine, had gone and told her that I am thinking of dating Aman.

Oh God. I'm dead.

2

THE (IN) SIGNIFICANT POEM COMPETITION

It was probably one of the longest walks of my life. Every time a teacher would call me, I knew it was because they wanted to praise my work, or just wanted to compliment me on something or the other. But with Gauri ma'am, my mind was always clouded, clueless about what to expect. So, when I reached her desk, I stood there, blank. Staring at her face, barely breathing.

After a while of hesitation, and complete silence, I finally asked, "Ma'am, you called for me?"

She suddenly jerked up in her seat, and looked away from her pile of sheets and said, "Yes...yes I did."

I felt beads of sweat roll down my face. *What is it woman! Can't you tell me already?*

"So, the thing is Sana..." She hesitated a little. *Oh God, this can't be good.*

"There's a very prestigious Poem writing competition coming up, and we can only send one entry from our school. And after a lot of contemplation, I have chosen you."

With fireworks bursting on the inside, a big awkward smile swept across my face.

"So, are you up for it Sana?" She asked irritated.

I felt like screaming, *duh! How can anyone say no to an offer like this, from YOU?* Instead, I said, "Yes, sure, ma'am. It would be my pleasure."

Now, let me explain why exactly this insignificant poem competition mattered to me so much. Truth be told, it was not about the competition, but about Gauri ma'am's acceptance. As I said before, just about every teacher adored me at FPS, except Gauri ma'am. And I wanted all, and by all, I meant *including* Gauri ma'am to like me, because each teacher vote mattered when it came to the very prestigious Middle School Student Council elections.

The Middle School Student Council, was basically something that I had been working towards since... probably a decade. *Okay, that may be a little over-exaggerated.* But, I had been working towards it since a very long time. Ever since I joined this school in fifth grade, I had been trying to get teachers and children to like me. I made sure to keep a clean reputation in front of the teachers, *no smoking, no drinking, no lovey-dovey stuff.* And it wasn't easy because of the fact that most of the students at FPS did all this. But I needed all those student and teacher votes, and I knew I had to make a sacrifice somewhere or the other.

As far as the student votes were concerned, they were set, but for the teachers votes, it was just Gauri ma'am who I was scared about. Well, I had finally gotten this opportunity to impress her, and I was determined to do my best and by that I meant I would do anything for winning this damn competition.

That day, as soon as I reached home, I headed straight to my room for I was determined to get things done. And now, all I needed was a little imagination and inspiration.

I live in 'Pinnacle' on the Golf Course Road and hence, the view from my room wasn't a pleasant one. The only thing visible was a swimming pool on the rooftop of one of the buildings which was painted in hues of blue and white. *Not the most inspiring view after all.*

As I began writing the first line, Mumma barged into the room looking as paranoid as ever.

Without looking up at her I uttered, "Mumma, I'm working on something very important here."

Although she was shorter than me, she could be very intimidating sometimes. Her eyes grew wider, and her soft smile disappeared.

"Beta this is not acceptable. At least go to the washroom to wash your face first!" She questioned me.

Without giving much consideration, I replied bluntly, "Mumma please let me work. It's Gauri Maam's work. Okay?"

Not saying a word further, she put the bowl of maggi on my table and paced out of the room, just as swiftly as she had come. She was furious already.

Honestly, while I portray my Mumma as the cruelest creature in this world, she isn't *that* bad. I mean, she can get excruciatingly angry sometimes, but she is a decent supportive forty-three-year-old lady, with some wrinkles here-and-there, hazelnut eyes and dark brown hair; who has always got your back. And to be honest, I'm quite similar in personality and character, when compared to my mom. At least, that's what I was always told.

It was another day all together when I woke up with the rays of Sun hitting my face, which was still resting on the study table from last night.

I recalled dozing off while working on the poem.

Ughhhh!

3

THE PRE-DATE DISTRACTIONS

The face of my phone glowed with white light shining brightly. My phone buzzed under my cheek, waking me up with the vibration. Half asleep, I quickly picked up the phone, without seeing who is calling.

"Hello?" I said, in a gruff tone.

A rather familiar voice replied, "Hey, it's me. Are you free to talk?"

Oh God! It's Aman. What was I supposed to do?

As for starters, I thought I shouldn't freak out. Also, I shouldn't calculate how long I've had a crush on him. And I should definitely not act at all weird. However, like always, I ended up doing all of the above, and it didn't turn out as I had planned. It turned out to be even better.

"Hey. I'm free...totally free...free like a bird. Tell me?"

I was clueless about what I was saying anymore. So, I immediately hung up the phone and carefully waited for him to text back. And the conversation was something like this...

Apart from the occasional stammering and repeating of words, the chat wasn't that bad.

Without even sparing a minute to think, I ran to the washroom. I had so much to do!

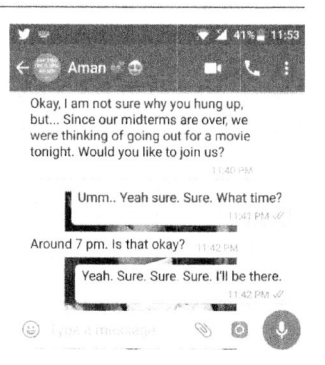

As the warm drops of water poured down on my bare skin, I closed my eyes and started to think of all the things that I had to do in the next seven hours. Although this may seem funny to the "god resides in mobile phones" generation, where but I always found the shower a spiritual place. It's where I can concentrate without worry.

But, I had so much on my mind. I didn't even have any dress in mind. My hair was all messed up and my face seemed dead. Once I was out of the shower, I followed the smell of some delicious iddlies which were being made by Mumma. I went straight to the kitchen, through the dining room.

"Mumma, I need to go for a movie with my friends tonight."

"Okay beta but-" She was interrupted by my Papa sitting on the dining table, with a cup of tea in one hand and a newspaper in the other.

My Papa is a good man but in our family, he's the stern one. While Mumma would easily agree to what I say, I need to provide Papa with a complete logical explanation for the minutest detail of the program. He was a little old, I mean, he appeared older than he was. He had this funny big-fat tummy, coupled with his twitching eyebrow and a short height, that often made it hard to take him seriously. But, he made sure, that he was taken seriously.

He spoke in his orotund voice, "So where are you headed tonight Sana?"

I slowly walked out of the kitchen, and prepared myself to face him. I replied in a soft tone, "Just for a movie with my friends. Since, our exams are finally over."

He seemed to examine my face for a second. As though, he is unveiling some deep dark hidden secret, and then after fifteen minutes of contemplation and extreme awkwardness, he said in his stern voice, "Okay, you can go. But come back soon Sana."

I didn't believe it for a second. He didn't ask me who I am going with, or which movie we're going for. He didn't ask which mall, which hall. And the numerous questions that follow. So, the only possibilities for that to happen are:

a. He is somehow in a good mood.
b. He hates me, and has given up on me. (even though I do everything he wants, and have often been called the 'perfect child')

One of the best moments of any female's life is probably when she steps out of a salon, just like a fresh cake out of an oven. My hair was washed and the hot curls seemed perfect. My eyebrows seemed 'on-point' quite literally, and my face was, as described by the package I chose "glowing and fresh." My nails were polished and in shape. All that pain that I bared, when that stranger, who I now hate, pulled off stripes of hot wax, from by naked skin; had finally paid off.

4

THE DATE

If I were to rate last night, it was a *ten-on-ten*. To begin with, as soon as I got there, dressed in a black dress (I know it was a little over done, for just a movie), I saw my minions standing and waiting for me. I took the lead and went up to the cinema hall. There, Ria was waiting for me with Rohan outside the box office. The only person missing – Aman.

For a second I felt like screaming my lungs out, and screeching in pain. I put in all this effort, for what? He didn't even show up! But all my fury was interrupted by Ria, "Sana, he's coming. He'll just be a little late."

That moment of relief, it can't be explained.

He turned up a few minutes before the interval. During the interval, both of us offered to go grab some snacks for the gang. We were walking towards the snack bar; a mere centimeter was the distance that kept our hands from touching. We finally reached the queue, and either of us were yet to say a word.

I could feel our bodies get tense, I could see that he was feeling awkward. And so, I started to brainstorm topics we could possibly talk about. The first topic that came to my mind was pancakes. I love pancakes, but *what if he hates them?* The next thing that I thought of was, dogs! I mean, who can *hate them?* And then it struck me, swimming.

"So, Aman, I saw you at the pool the other day."

"Yeah. Umm...I like to swim. What about you?"

Well, I don't know, I haven't ever really thought of swimming as...swimming. I just took it as something that you've got to bunk because you're a girl. I mean, I think the last time I entered the pool was like last year.

"Oh...I love swimming." Wait, why did I say that? Oh God.

He seemed stunned. And he probably understood that I was lying. But he hesitantly asked, "So, do you... swim professionally too?"

Duh no. Why did I lie? Why did I get into this mess?

"Well, I haven't really thought about that...Could you train me? I mean I've seen you swim, and you win almost every race."

A middle-age paranoid man pushed me from the back and said, "Young lady, can you please move. It's your turn." And that is how our somehow-intimate chat was disturbed by an old man who was in a rush to gobble down some popcorn.

But, it wasn't over yet. As we walked back to the Audi, with hands full of food, he finally broke the silence by replying to my question.

"About what you said, a. I am not *that* good. and b. I guess, yes, I can train you."

My red colored lips stretched across my face as soon as he said that. Is this a dream?

He continued, "But...probably once school is closed for summer break, because, the pool these days is very busy and full."

I think he could see that I was disappointed, because my smile vanished, and so did my dimples. So, he further made his point by saying in a soft tone, "Well it's just a matter of a few days, and that way, we'll have the whole pool to ourselves."

"Yes. I wouldn't mind waiting a while," I said softly.

We both smiled in sync at each other, and then looked away as we entered the hall. As I sat there inside, in complete darkness, I barely watched the movie, and that's probably the reason why I couldn't answer to Papa when he asked me this morning, "How was the movie, should we watch it too?

Throughout, I kept taking peeks from the corner of my eye at his perfect silhouette. I could smell his strong perfume that suited him just fine. I could hear him breathe in my ears, I could see him smile.

5

MAY 13TH, 2017

Today was the day when one of the most anticipated results were to come out. The selection for the Middle School Student council of Florens Public School. The results for the student council mattered to the students more than the 10th Grade board exams, beyond whether India won the India-Pakistan cricket match, because these were the results which would tell us who would basically rule Middle School for the coming year. Most importantly, it'll decide who won the competition for which we had all been fighting from the day we entered Middle School in 6th Grade.

And I just couldn't wait.

So, as soon as our buses stopped at the entrance of the school, I picked up my bag, and raced up the two flights of stairs, to get to our floor. By the time I reached the Middle School floor, huffing and puffing, I noticed the big disappointed crowd gathered in front of our head, Ms. Preeti's room. They were all hovering around the notice board where the results were to be released, and it seemed that it was empty.

Renuka, one of my minions told me that according to a rumor, the results will be out only after lunch.

Wow, now I had to wait till lunch? That's like telling a hungry child that you've got to starve until eternity. Okay, maybe not the best metaphor, but my point has been made.

Our first lesson was Mathematics with one of the shortest teacher's in history – Deepika ma'am. A rumor has it that she used to earlier carry a portable stool around, so that she could get on it and write on the board.

Although I pretty much love Maths, that day, I just couldn't wait. I simply wanted to press some sort of fast forward button to skip past all the boring lessons and go for lunch and then see the results. But that was obviously not possible. So, once the loud bell rang, we all paced out of the room, and headed straight to Gauri Maam's class.

We sat in our usual spots in Gauri ma'am's class, but this time, we weren't playing any game. For some reason, silence had made way into the classroom and sat staring at us creepily whispering in our ears words that made no sense but affected our heartbeats. The anticipation was about to kill me.

The kids with the large specs and freckled faces, in other words, the geeks, who weren't talking about some mysterious science expedition. Instead, they were simply staring at the wall in front. The kids with the scars and the blank expressions weren't doing anything stupid either. Instead, they too were all quiet. And the cool kids, aka us, were, as I like to put it, sat there as quiet as dead bodies. Yet again, not the best metaphor, my apologies.

And the funniest thing was that Gauri ma'am was late for class. Yes, Gauri ma'am, the perfectionist who had never, in the history of FPS school, been absent or late for a class.

So, I thought to myself, this better be good. And it was indeed.

6

BEST. DAY. EVER.

The wooden door to the classroom banged open and at the entrance stood Gauri Ma'am with a certificate in hand. She seemed as though she had just gone under a 120 volts shock treatment because her hair was mostly standing up, her white teeth were all showing through as she gave us the biggest smile. Her eyes were open wide, and so were her hands. And she was looking straight at me.

"You won!" She yelled with joy.

Wait, is she seriously looking at me? Is she talking to me? What did I…win?

"You won the poem competition Sana! You won!"

That moment, I realized what was going on. I won the freaking poem competition for which I worked my ass off. Oh God, could I be happier? (I mean I could…If I win the Student Council elections…but we'll get to that later).

Soon, I noticed that she was still standing with her hands stretched out towards me, so I daringly took my steps towards her and as soon as I reached her, she engulfed me by wrapping around her oddly long hands. I think at some point, she also attempted to pick me up, but couldn't (not because I'm fat, she was just a little weak).

I could feel all eyes staring at us. I could feel my heartbeat increase... And I knew that more good things were yet to come. I graciously smiled at ma'am and hear her say how proud she was for me. It was a moment of happiness and I felt like nothing could take it away from me.

They say all good things take time, and so, Gauri Maam's acceptance towards me took its own sweet time. But now that it had ultimately happened, the feeling of achievement was inexpressible.

After the English lesson, we were going for lunch. I have earlier described our dining hall as magnificent and mammoth like. But what I didn't narrate is how to get there and what all can happen in that brief five-minute journey.

Minute 1

The road that goes from our main school building to our dining hall seemed mystical. On both sides of the road were tall palm trees with some big trees fallen from their branches. Behind these palm trees, on both sides were vast green fields from where one could still smell the lingering petrichor because it was still raining. Adding to the above detail were the end bits of the low-lying Aravalli ranges in the far background.

Ria and I were walking towards the dining hall, when Aman approached us.

The Burning Truth

Minute 2

It seemed like he had run all the way from the second floor to us, because he was panting and sweating a lot, which made his shirt stick to his body, enhancing his perfect physique. For a second, I got transported to this dream-world where Aman and I were sitting on a cute swing in the middle of a lush green park. My thoughts were disturbed by Aman's words.

"Hey Ria..."

Wait a minute. *Is he here to talk to Ria? All this while I had been thinking... Oh God. What a mess. WHAT A MESS!*

By this point, I had stopped hearing what he was saying, because, quite honestly, I was burning with fire on the inside. So, when I saw Ria go away, and turn and pass me a wink, leaving me and Aman all alone on the path, I was startled. *What was even happening? Why do I zone out so often?*

Minute 3

I tried to act all cool, and so I asked looking straight at him, "Oh, so you've come to talk to...me?"

He hesitantly replied, "Yeah Sana, who else?"

Note to self, never zone out in a situation such as this.

I had already made a fool of myself. And so, I replied, "Umm...no one. So, you were...saying?"

Minute 4

Oh, this was the minute when both of us got too awkward to say anything. And so, this minute was spent in complete silence.

Minute 5

He finally broke the silence by grabbing me by one hand and turning me swiftly, to face him. He then directed me to sit on the staircase outside, that led to the dining hall, and we sat there in the drizzling rain, clutching each other's hands.

7

KILIG

A drop of rain trickled down my face, and I felt this glittery feeling within. Now, I knew what feeling kilig was like.

He looked deep into my eyes, and said, "Look, I know this might be all too fast for you, but I really like you. I had…earlier thought to wait until school closes for break. I had not really planned on asking you out right now. But the thing is… I can't wait. I just can't wait to spend whatever time we have left together. And I don't want to waste a single moment."

At that moment, it seemed as though the world was moving in fast motion, while we just sat there, paused.

I had no reply at hand. I just sat with my mouth half open, speechless. I could feel my cheeks go red, and I knew that my dimples were very evident by now. I leaned in a little closer to him and said, "So…umm, what is this?"

"I… I don't know if this is a proposal, but I do know that I can't live another minute without you by my side."

For a second, I was confused and I could tell, so was he.

I took a lock of my hair, and tugged it behind my ear. I then gently rubbed my thumb on the front of his hand, it felt like I am consoling him for some reason. All this while, I was staring at our wet shoes, and now, I finally looked up, and into his dark brown eyes, and I could feel my heart glow. All this gave me a little time to digest all that was fed into my brain in the last few seconds.

In a voice, that was almost softer than a whisper I replied, "I don't think I would like to live another second without you Aman."

And that was our moment.

I was overwhelmed with all that had happened on the 13th of May. It felt like nothing could possibly go wrong that day. To begin with, Gauri Ma'am actually came and *hugged me.* Then, a guy on who I had a crush on since... I don't know...like forever, finally asked me out in such a cute (and impromptu!) way that I couldn't really describe at that point.

Perhaps, I pretty much felt invincible. As though, God's complete attention is on me. I really had a good feeling about the student council results too. I mean, if I managed to become the Head Girl for Middle School, which is basically the queen of Middle School, then this day would be a successful hattrick!

So, after lunch, Ria and I rushed to the school building through the puddles on the road, with our favorite salad bar food item – some sort of street food, filled in glasses. By the time we reached back, our once perfectly white shoes had turned perfectly brown.

The Burning Truth

Hardly giving a damn, we continued to run upstairs and when we reached the pink noticeboard, we could barely see a thing because of the enormous crowd. So, Ria being the rough-and-tough one in our friendship, grabbed me by my hand and navigated me through the crowd, pushing aside everyone else, till we reached up front. By now I was covered in sweat, and could feel the heavy breathing and pressure of all those who were trying to crush us.

"Oh Ria, better watch out dude," screamed a guy we nearly knocked down.

"Omesh, you need to watch out and watch down, before you fall down the next time. Now, you better shut up bro," she shouted back.

As we finally reached the pink noticeboard, I saw an almost crushed, white page with coffee spills and hand prints with two columns drawn. One which said position, while the other that stated the name of the person who was given that position. I barely had the guts to look at the sheet with the results. The results...for which I had stayed up on endless nights. The results that meant everything to me at that moment. So, instead of reading the list, I simply looked away and closed my eyes.

"I can't look at it. I'm...too scared."

I could feel that she was irritated, "What do you mean by, you can't look at it. Just open your eyes and see!"

8

WOLF IN A SHEEP'S SKIN

I knew there was no escaping from this. So, I slowly opened my eyes, which revealed a list of names and positions pinned to the board.

My eyes first went to Aman's name. He had got the position of Head of Sports. That was regarded as an honorable job indeed, though I was expecting him to become Head Boy or something. Anyway, congratulations to him, he at least got into the Student Council. Next, I noticed Ria's name, and she was our new head of technology, I was impressed.

I then scanned through the entire list once again, I had begun to panic on still

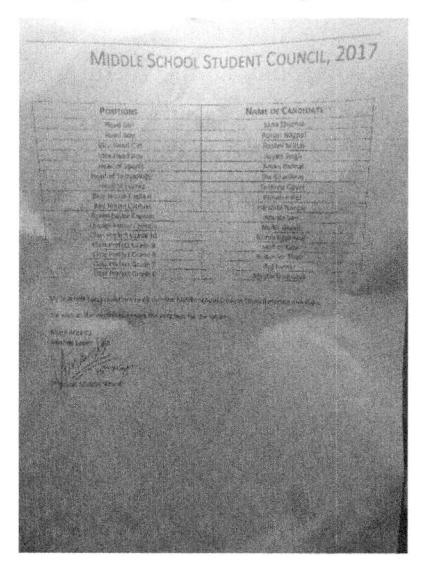

The Burning Truth

not finding my name. My eyes grew big, and my body began sweating. I could feel my hands shivering and I knew that this wasn't good.

"Sana, congratulations!" Ria shouted.

"For what Ria? my name isn't there." I replied.

She seemed a little irritated, but happy at the same time.

"Oh God you dumbo! Yours is the first name on the list. You are our new head girl!" She informed me enthusiastically.

I couldn't believe it, and I think it was all too much for me, though I had been expecting the same from deep within. My little brain couldn't take it all and so I blacked out.

When I woke up, the first thing that my eyes saw was Aman, sitting by my bed holding my hand tight. How is he already such a good boyfriend? What did I do to deserve a guy like him? Then I noticed it wasn't just him. In the dimly lit room, with colorful curtains and white walls, in the corner I saw that Ria and my gang were waiting in the seating area as well. At that moment, I realized how blessed I truly was.

❀ ❀ ❀

Later, at the bus stop when I stepped down from the bus, Mumma greeted me with a big smile. So, I presumed, that she somehow got to know about the good things that had happened to me today, perhaps Goyal Aunty, our neighbor who is also a teacher at our school had told her.

Or maybe, the results had been published online. Anyway, I was certain that she knew about me getting the head girl position and winning the competition, and so, I went along with it. As soon as we got home, Mumma grabbed my bag and threw it onto the sofa. She then clutched me by the arms, and hugged me so tight, that for a second it felt as though I am going to lose control and blackout again.

When I finally managed to pull away, I asked, "Thank you Mumma. I know you're always happy with whatever I manage to do, but I hope Papa is happy too...you know?"

She seemed a little puzzled, but then she replied, "Oh Sana, he is happy for you. He is so happy! In fact, he has said that once he returns tomorrow morning, he would congratulate you in person, not over the phone."

Okay, now it was me who was confused. "Are you serious Mumma?"

"Yes darling, of course I am serious."

I was taken aback a little. *My father was happy? With something that... I had achieved? Was he okay?* But then, although he wouldn't be happy about Aman, two good news in one day, is something too. So maybe...he too, is happy. And thinking this, I smiled back at her and went to my room.

❀ ❀ ❀

It felt like I am suffocating. I breathed heavily, trying to inhale as much of air, as possible; but I failed. I could barely see in the pitch darkness of the room. The only source of light visible to my naked eye was a candle burning far away in the distance. It seemed so far, that the flame almost seemed like a blob of orange and yellow color.

The Burning Truth

I tried to follow the flame visible far away, but it seemed as though with each step I took, the distance between us increased. It felt like I am on this endless treadmill which resisted me from reaching the flame. And the flame seemed like my only hope and my only way to get out of that endless dark room that seemed to have trapped me in itself.

I slowly paced my steps, one following the other. Trying to make my way, following the light. And then suddenly, I felt as if I was falling.

While I lay there, flat on my stomach, facing down, my hair flew upwards. My clothes had gradually begun to come off, possibly due to the high air pressure. There was water all around me, I could see it clearly, yet I couldn't feel it. I was falling at such a high speed, yet I didn't feel any air press against my bare skin. I couldn't feel anything at all.

I tried to scream for *help* but it came out hardly as a whisper. I shouted again, but there was no one out there. And then, slowly, I saw the water disappear. While I was falling downwards, it seemed to travel in the opposite direction, something that is truly against natural science.

And that's when I saw them. Mumma and Papa, standing at the other end of the endless hole. They were there. They were watching me fall. They were watching me, yet they simply stood there, leaving me feel helpless. I screamed in fear, "Help me Mumma! Don't just keep looking! Help me please!"

When she failed to respond I shouted with all the energy I was left with, "I'm falling Papa! Pull me out of this hole! I'm falling and I can't breathe. Mumma, Papa... *Help me get out of this hole!"*

"Sana, what happened beta? Are you okay?" shouted my Mumma dressed in her loose night wear, with her hair spread all across her face. She shook me with all her might, attempting to wake me up.

I forced my eyes open, and asked her, "I – I ...don't know what happened. It felt like I am falling...and falling and it just kept going. The worst part was...I could see you Mumma...but you-you didn't help me."

"Oh beta, do you actually believe that it's possible for you to be in pain, and I don't help you?" she said in a surprised tone.

"I don't know. It was just a nightmare I think. I'll be... fine. Don't worry." I said with my hands still shivering under the covering sheet.

But she seemed barely convinced, probably because my words were still sloppy and my eyes seemed red. My hair resembled the hair of a witch, and my body seemed cold.

So, she stayed there for a while, stroking my hair. And after some time, when she thought I'm asleep she silently exited the room.

But I lay there awake, barely moving or breathing. And that's when I realized, all these good things that had been happening to me one after the other, perhaps they were the wolf in a sheep's skin.

And regardless of how happy I was about all the good things, at this point, I couldn't have been more scared about the storm coming my way.

9

THE "GOOD" NEWS

It was nine in the morning when I finally woke up because of the knock on the door. It was Papa, I knew that because I could see his shiny jet-black shoes through the slit under the door.

"I'll just come in two minutes Papa. I need to go to the washroom first." I mumbled with my eyes half-open.

"Alright Sana. But come quick, I have good news." He said excitedly.

I thought I was the one who was to give the good news about student council and the competition... What is he talking about? Or maybe...he just feels that my good news is his good news, or some sort of that parental crap.

Later, I went outside my room, to our dining table, where Mumma and Papa were seated. They seemed so delighted, even Papa *(for a change).* I pushed back the heavy wooden chair making a creaky sound, but I chose not to sit. Instead I smiled and said, "So, before you both say anything, I would like to thank you for your constant support throughout my journey at FPS, till date. And I am sure that you would continue to love and support me in my journey forward."

Papa then stood up, pushing back his chair, and motioning for me to sit down. "We are proud of you Sana. And yes, we would support you no matter what, be it FPS or Avenues International School."

Wait what? What did he just say? *Avenues international school?* It felt like my world had been turned upside down. I didn't know what was happening, how did that snooty school come into the picture of me becoming head girl and winning a poem competition?

I needed to stay calm, I told myself. Maybe I am just not clear with what Papa was saying, I thought. So, in a voice as calm as possible, I asked, "Sorry, what did you say Papa?"

He seemed certain of what he said, "You heard me Sana, I said we'll be there for you even when…you shift to Avenues International school."

By now it hit me. And I couldn't stay calm. So, in an almost screaming tone, I replied, "Wait a minute, so are you saying that…you are changing my school to Avenues International?"

My Mumma seemed baffled by now, she asked, "Sana, I thought you knew beta. That is why I was congratulating you yesterday…remember?"

"Of course, I remember. But what I don't recall, is you telling me that I am supposed to change schools." I screamed at her sarcastically.

"I thought you knew somehow. Otherwise, why would you come down from the bus, so happy?"

The Burning Truth

And that's when it all made sense. Mumma didn't even know about the Aman thing, and neither was she aware about the student council or the competition. Now, I understood why Papa was filled with joy as well. It wasn't about *me* winning the competition. Or about *me* becoming the head girl. He was only delighted because *he* managed to get my admission in that snobbish international school.

Papa looked at me with his stern face, as though he could read my mind, and was disappointed with what I was *thinking.* After giving me the disappointed look, he finally said, "Look, it seems like there has been some misunderstanding, so, let me make the facts crystal clear."

Before he could finish, for the first time in my lifetime, I interrupted him and said, "Let me make something clear here. I got into the student council as the *Head Girl, at FPS!* And all this while, I thought that both of you even knew that. I won a poem competition which is extremely exclusive and I had the best day of my life yesterday."

I could see that Papa's forehead was now full of lines of tension, his eyes seemed to expand, and then, he ruffled his own hair with one hand, a thing which he does when he is about to scold someone.

He looked at me and firmly told me, "Okay Sana. That's good if you had the best day of your merely-15 years of life, but you need to understand that we have changed your school, for your betterment–"

I cut him off, "No, you did not, I mean you never even asked me!"

"We are your parents Sana, and we know what's best for you. I got a promotion at job and so we want to give you a better education. No further discussion on this. We are done here." He shut me down with that.

Without waiting for a second, I simply turned around and ran back to my room, as I entered through the doors, I heard Papa say, "Tomorrow morning, at eight, we need to go and talk to the principal to clear the final round. Now, you may go and spend the rest of the day in your room."

I shut the door on his face. And that was it.

That was all the explanation I received.

10

FLUSHED DOWN THE TOILET

Papa was right, I had spent the entire day in my room, thinking about things that were of no relevance now, because the decision was already made, *by my parents.*

As I sat on my bed and stared at the wall, with my hair open, in loose pajamas, I contemplated about all the things that I had at FPS, things that took time and effort to achieve. Now, I will have to restart all over on a clean slate at Avenues.

Things such as, my enormous, almost never-ending social circle; the *(little)* respect and *(lots of)* love from my juniors and seniors; the appreciation my teachers had for me; the position of head girl I had achieved; a perfect relationship; my reputation and just about everything that I had worked for since fourth grade, was being flushed down the toilet.

When I finally got out of my room for dinner, I decided to have a calm conversation, which was more of me talking and them listening, with my parents who were seated in front of the Plasma TV, watching "*Sara bhai vs Sara bhai,*" in the living room. I had prepared a long speech which I had practiced exactly thirty-three times for perfecting my voice modulation, and for adequate emotions that were to be exhibited.

So, to draw all attention to myself, I went and stood right in front of the TV, to block their view. I immediately got their attention, perhaps because I was blocking their view. And, before they could say anything, I began speaking.

"What happened today, made me reconsider and ponder about my past four years at Florens Public School. And I concluded, I was hurt about a. you not even slightly appreciating me for becoming the head girl. b. you are changing my school without considering all that I had worked for but most importantly" I was shredding tears by now. "Most importantly – you not even thinking of taking my opinion on such a life-changing decision.

I realized that I was extremely hurt about having to leave this school where I was quite honestly, enjoying a great social, academic and love life, but I was even more hurt... that my parents-" I could barely control the feelings anymore and so I started to sob like a little baby. "I was even more hurt that...my parents hardly cared about all of this."

By the end of my speech, I expected at least an apology from Mumma for not even considering or hearing my opinion and at least a nod from Papa. Instead what I got was, Mumma saying, "we're doing what's best for you." And Papa, literally not reacting at all.

That was when I realized, they are really going through with this decision. And no matter what, be it me locking myself up in my room, or giving them a long ass emotional speech, their decision was rock solid and nothing could change.

All I wanted... all I was looking for was an explanation for the big change in my life without my consent.

During the evening, when Papa had gone for his daily walk, I went to Mumma's room to ask her why had they done this. I knocked lightly on the door and entered the velvet colored room that belonged to my parents. I found Mumma seated on her bed, reading a book.

When she saw me, she looked up and passed me a soft smile, that seemed full of pity and perhaps some love. So, I finally pulled myself together and asked her, "Mumma, why are you doing this? Why didn't you ask me, or at least tell me before applying for my admission?"

She patted the bed, directing me to sit next to her. I jumped aboard, like a little girl. Her words still resonate in my ears, and are hard to forget, "Sana, we are your family, we are married to each other until death does us all apart. But the friends for whom you are willing to fight for now... they are temporary and they will... you believe it or not, eventually...fade away. But the ones who stay, are keepers.

So, if that is what is killing you so much, then beta it's fine. In few years from now, you would barely remember their faces or names. And about the part where we didn't ask for your opinion, we really did it only for your best, because we knew you wouldn't want to leave a place where you are the queen. But we know you'll thank us later, because trust me, it's only delusional to be a figure among cyphers."

At that point, only 10% of her speech made sense, and I was still hurt. So, even after listening to her, I was barely convinced, and so I smiled, did the ceremonious south Indian nod, and saw myself out. As I was about to leave, she said one last thing, "Remember one thing, we love you beta."

I didn't reply, and went back to my room only partially satisfied, only if I had known what was in stock for me the next morning, I would've acted all differently.

11

THE GAME AT AVENUES

The next morning, Mumma, Papa and I drove to Avenues International School, Gurgaon for my interview with the Principal of Middle School.

When we reached the main doors of the school, I was stunned. It was truly, a jaw dropping moment. For a second I fantasized the school as a modern palace with glass windows and a chic design. Instead of horse ridden carriages, there stood club carts at the entrance. In front of the main building, was a gigantic field that resemble the one I had seen in films like 'Student of the Year.'

As we climbed up a few steps that lead us to the lobby, there were two magnificent fountains that were flowing on both our sides. When we finally entered the main lobby, a bright red signboard with an Avenues logo, and a lady with her hands folded, welcomed us.

For a second I was startled, and I pondered was this a hotel or a school? The crystal-clear floor, the glassed cabins, the leafy plants and most importantly, the staff, in my opinion, were all comparable to that of a luxury hotel.

I had stood in the center of the hall admiring the scale model of the school which showcased three humongous buildings covered in a pale ceramic color, a vast field that would probably be used for football, four courts that were either utilized for tennis or badminton, and three other basketball courts. Although it all seemed glorious, one thing seemed missing, the swimming pool!

I spotted where Mumma and Papa were standing and ran to them to tell them the one negative point I found about this school, the missing swimming pool.

But as I went and told them, the sharp looking lady, dressed in a jet-black suit, who was our chaperone explained, "Good morning Sana, allow me to answer your concern. I believe your question arises after looking at the scale model. Actually, we have an underground, basement-level, centrally heated swimming pool. Since it is inside the main building, you were unable to see it in the model."

With that, the one downside that I had found in the picturesque Avenues school, was proven false.

Then I had a eureka moment. *If* I must study at this school and the decision *has* been made; then what is even the point in trying to find negatives about this place? And *if* I really wanted to leave this building without a final admission, my only hope was to act funnily and dumb in front of the principal.

As we climbed up a flight of stairs, I thought of all the possible things I could do so that she would decide not to give me admission. I could probably start scratching my leg like a mad animal, or I could start exercising in

The Burning Truth

between of the meeting because "my legs feel sore" or the simplest, I would not answer anything she asks me, or I'll just give absurd answers.

We waited outside the Principal's office for about fifteen minutes before she called us inside. I could see that Papa was a little irritated because he had frowns on his forehead, and was continuously tapping his feet. Mumma was a little restless too, but that was probably because we ate oily food for breakfast.

That day, when we entered the spacious, clean room, I saw a leather cushioned chair kept on one side of the room, behind a dark brown modular table. In the other half of the room were low rise, white colored sofas on which we were requested to sit on.

The fifty-something principal, who was dressed in a dull black and white printed sari, had straight salt-and-pepper hair which were neatly put in place. She paced towards us, with a big smile and a hand jutting forward, for a handshake.

This was my first opportunity to defy my parents and the principal. Although I knew she was expecting a handshake from me, I simply sat there, waiting for Papa to rise instead. Both Mumma and Papa stared at me with stern faces for few seconds, and then, after giving up, they chose to smile and shake hands with her instead.

Point 1 came to me.

Firstly, she introduced herself, "Good afternoon Mr. and Mrs. Sharma. I am Ms. Anshoo Gupta, Principal of the Middle Years Programme, at Avenues International School."

All three of us simply smiled.

"So, I believe that Sana Sharma, here, is enrolling for Year 4 at Avenues International."

I think she expected a nod, or a yes or something at least from me. But instead, I had chosen to simply look at the magazines on the table in front of our sofa. She negated my reaction and continued.

Point 2 again to...me?

"Mr. and Mrs. Sharma, today's interview would include two sections. The first where I talk about Avenues, and the second where you talk about why I should let you be a part of Avenues. So, let's begin!"

Papa finally responded, "Sure Ms. Gupta."

"To begin with, at Avenues International School, we believe that every child is unique and special. I tell each parent who brings their child to this school that we are different, because we are an IB school, and so we have our own philosophy."

We all nodded in synchronization.

"Our ideology is simple, don't just study. Enjoy it, our only criterion for choosing children is one: Uniqueness. Now I would like you to speak Sana. So, tell me a little about yourself."

That was my turn to ruin every possible chance of being in that wonderful school. What I planned to say was, "I don't really think there's much to tell about myself. I personally feel I'm perfect, but this school isn't. So, it's not about you choosing me, it's about me choosing you." But then, I had felt like my tongue went numb and I couldn't utter a word. I couldn't say what I wanted to.

Instead I smiled, sat upright, and said, "Ms. Gupta, to begin with, I want to say, that I am no stellar student, although I topped in my last school – Florens Public School, Gurgaon. Yet I am unique, in many ways. I have managed to juggle well between extra-curricular and academics in the past few years. And my only moto to come here is to develop and grow into a better human being."

Point 3 won't come to me.

What had happened? My hands were shivering and I had goosebumps. I could feel my head spinning. It felt like my fighter instincts just woke up and said all that. Because, that is not what I had planned to say.

I could make out that, Ms. Gupta was also quite surprised because she was staring at me as though I am a person who rose from the dead. She smiled and said, "Well Sana, I think that was all I needed to hear. Welcome to Avenues International."

And that was it.

I don't know what happened there, I really don't, but I had begun to have a good feeling about all this, all of a sudden.

12

THE LIES

Now that we had finalized my admission at Avenues International School, I decided it's time to break up with Aman, because long distances don't work and are pointless due to the constant trauma that one of them would either cheat or lose interest. So, that night, after I got into my bed and under the comfortable blanket, I took out my phone to text him.

I opened WhatsApp, and the first name that appeared was Aman.

So, I clicked on it, and I started to type, but my hands were full of sweat because of all the stress and tension. I wiped them onto the bed cover and then continued typing. His reply took even less than a minute.

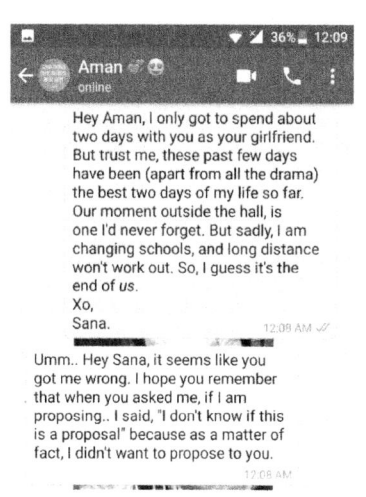

> Hey Aman, I only got to spend about two days with you as your girlfriend. But trust me, these past few days have been (apart from all the drama) the best two days of my life so far. Our moment outside the hall, is one I'd never forget. But sadly, I am changing schools, and long distance won't work out. So, I guess it's the end of *us*.
> Xo,
> Sana.

> Umm.. Hey Sana, it seems like you got me wrong. I hope you remember that when you asked me, if I am proposing.. I said, "I don't know if this is a proposal" because as a matter of fact, I didn't want to propose to you.

The Burning Truth

I was up in flames the minute I saw that. I mean, *what does he mean by 'I didn't want to propose to you?'* If he didn't want to, then why did he choose to grab me and tell me that 'he couldn't live another minute without me' and all that nonsense. *What was all that for huh?* I wanted to say all these things, and so this time, I did. I texted him back.

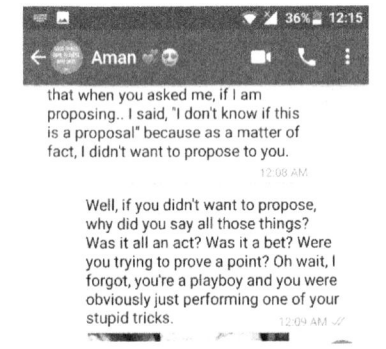

> that when you asked me, if I am proposing.. I said, "I don't know if this is a proposal" because as a matter of fact, I didn't want to propose to you.
>
> Well, if you didn't want to propose, why did you say all those things? Was it all an act? Was it a bet? Were you trying to prove a point? Oh wait, I forgot, you're a playboy and you were obviously just performing one of your stupid tricks.

And once I sent him that, I never texted him again for a long-long time. I blocked him from every social media, and I blocked him from my life too, or at least so had I thought.

That same night, I also texted Ria telling her that I won't be coming to FPS because I was changing my school. She didn't reply, but I was sure she soon would. So, just to double check, I texted her on every other social media account I possibly could, Snapchat, Instagram, Facebook Messenger and *even WeChat*.

The next morning, I woke up with swollen eyes and plump cheeks. This was a common thing that happened every time I cried at night. So, when I went outside my room for breakfast, the first thing Mumma asked was, "Did you cry last night?" I looked around to check if Papa was around but he wasn't and so I decided to tell her everything.

I started by telling her about the whole story about Aman and how he betrayed me and played with my mind.

I then also told her about how I would really miss all my friends from FPS, and that I was still waiting for Ria to reply.

This time, she hadn't given me a dose of her wise words of wisdom. Instead, she smiled and heard me ramble about all the miseries of my life. Once I was done, she took me to the drawing room and calmly asked me to sit down. As I did, she took out her phone from her back pocket and opened images of Avenues International School saying, "Look Sana, you're going to this wonderful, better school which has things such as golf and horse riding. Now, just...remember it's okay. Aman would be soon erased from your memory. But what you need to focus on right now is...that your first day of school is tomorrow, and you should look perfect."

I nodded and went back to my room, to take out my uniform and set my bag. That day, I checked my phone at intervals of fifteen minutes, but Ria didn't reply. And I knew, this wasn't going to end well.

13

THE NEW (UNI)FORM

At six in the morning, the alarm started to buzz. I turned it off, and got back into the comfort of my cozy bed. After a while, at six fifteen, my phone started to vibrate, I snoozed that too and tried to go back to sleep. Ultimately, Mumma had barged into my room joyfully screaming, "It's your first day at Avenues! Wake up Sana!"

And that was precisely the reason I didn't want to wake up. So, I pulled my blanket over my head, trying to make sure that no sunlight got into my eyes. "I am not getting out of my bed today Mumma. Leave. Me. Alone!"

She then used her final tactic – I saw her coming out of my bathroom with a mug full of water, which I knew she would pour on me. So, as soon as one drop of that ice-chilled water touched my skin, I rose with a thud, throwing away my blanket, screaming in annoyance "Alright alright, you win Mumma, I'm getting out of bed, okay?!"

I got out of bed and ran into the washroom. I sat and slept for at least half an hour before Mumma came banging on the door shouting, "Get out of there! You can't be late for the first day of your new school Sana!" And with that, my last minute of peace in the washroom came to an end. I rushed out and put on the new uniform that was lying on the bed, folded neatly.

I recall seeing myself for the first time in the new uniform, it was different. I tied my straight hair up in a high ponytail, and put on some lip balm making my lips look seemingly full. My hazelnut eyes seemed weak and tired due to all the crying, and yet, oddly enough they were full of life.

I picked up my bag and went outside the room, when Mumma who was sitting on the table looked up and said, "Oh Sana, you look so smart....and intellectual. These shorts and t-shirt suit you just fine. I've packed you a banana and you can eat it in the bus. Okay?"

She seemed so delighted, for reasons I couldn't comprehend. I hugged her tight, and said "Alright Mumma. I will eat it. And don't worry, I'll do just fine."

"I know you will," she said so confidently that it was quite motivating. I looked at her one last time, as I walked out of the main door.

❀ ❀ ❀

A completely different system was followed in my new school-bus – AIS 13. Unlike my last bus, where all the cool kids like me got to sit in the four-seater. In this bus, there were no four seats. It was a simple plain old bus with two seats in one row, and three seats in the other. I recollected that the older students sat at the back of the bus, and so I thought that the same would be followed here too.

My bus stop was the first, so I went to the back rows of the bus as I had the freedom to choose. I sat on my chosen two-seater, with my bag placed next to me. I sat there, waiting for the bus to move, when it did, I took out my bright yellow banana shaped case which my mom had kept for me.

Barely two minutes had passed when the bus came to a halt at the next stop – The Icon, and a group of little kids, with pigtails and small water bottles began to climb onto the bus. The nanny took their bags and placed them onto the seats. Then came in the teenagers. The first girl who entered the bus had dark brown curly hair with golden highlights. She was much taller than me, and had headphones on. As she walked passed me, I first thought she didn't notice me but then I saw her staring at me from literally the corner of her eye, and, it was scary.

But who cares? Right?

I had chosen to continue to peel my banana, one strip at a time. And after taking a few turns, we paused at DLF Camellias. For a moment no one had entered, and then, as I took my second bite, a group of tall teenagers swamped the bus.

The first guy who entered seemed geeky with a laptop in hand and large spectacles on his nose. He also had a badge hanging on his t-shirt that read "Tech Head." The next guy that entered was wearing the wrong shoes (*on the first day???*) and an Armani belt which was again wrong, he had blonde highlights in one section of his hair. They were followed by a couple of third or perhaps fourth graders, and then a short girl entered the bus.

She seemed like a nice person, because she was wearing glasses, and had a couple of heavy books in one hand. Her eyes were big and dark, she had extremely straight hair, and was quite short. Her face was oval and resembled an egg, but overall, she looked like a cute little doll.

I could tell that she was confused as to where to sit, because she was looking at each seat at the back, so I offered her the seat next to me. And she had graciously accepted it. Silence followed between us, because I was eating my banana, finally she asked, "Are you new here?" I quickly finished what was in my mouth and replied, "Yes, and you?" she said, she was new too. This had made me happy.

Since I wasn't the only 'new kid' and there were more people. I soon learnt that her name was Deepali and she's come from a boarding school in Shimla. As we continued to talk, time passed by quickly and before I knew it, a not too tall guy with peculiar black hair, a funny smile, and dark brown eyes entered the bus. He seemed full of energy even on a Monday morning. He threw away his bag into the top shelf which was above our heads, and started to move towards the back of the bus. He greeted almost every little kid as he came forward by asking silly things like "what did you eat for dinner?" or "How was your night" and high fiving everyone at the same time.

When he approached us, he looked at us as though we were some sort of aliens who had entered his territory without his permission. He examined the girl sitting next to me, and said in a caustic tone, "You seem like a nerd, you go away and let me sit here." I looked at him and tried to give him the death stare, but he remained unaffected and in no time, he had taken the place of the new girl and was now sitting next to me.

I wanted to look unresponsive, so instead of paying attention to his next actions, I continued to eat my banana. And that's when I noticed he was staring at me with his dark brown eyes. I couldn't take it anymore so I asked him, "Dude what are you doing? And why did you tell her to leave?"

He looked back at all the other seniors and gave them a quirky smile, and then he finally replied, "You first tell me, who eats a banana in the bus?" Before I had the time to react, it felt like the entire bus was laughing at me. I imagined standing on a stage in a big auditorium, where me and my dignity were being stripped off in front of everyone. They all stared at me, and giggled or laughed like monsters.

But what did I do?

As he rose to move away, he ducked once again and whispered in my ear, "A piece of advice, next time, don't eat a banana in a public place." He passed me a ribald wink and went back to take a seat. I obviously quickly put back the banana into my case and kept it into my rose-printed bag.

As we drove towards the school, through the hills, I thought about why everyone found me eating a banana so comical. *It just made zero sense, until I reached home and saw what it means on urban dictionary.*

Finally, my disastrous bus ride came to an end as we had reached Avenues International School. Even though I had had a rough start, I felt this won't be just that bad. After all, not all schools have facilities like a heated indoor swimming pool. I waited for everyone to step down from the bus, so that I was the last one to leave. When I did, I could still feel eyes trying to peer into my soul and rip apart my skin.

I realized Deepali was still waiting for me to come walk with her to school and so I kept my head high, and walked straight towards her, with my bag hung on my right shoulder. On our way to the main building I told her about how he was trying to make fun of me and I had no clue what was happening. She too giggled a little as we walked up the flight of stairs that led us to the floor that was for Grade 9 students as told by Ms. Gupta. Somehow, she knew where her class was, and so, off she went.

Now, the only problem was... *Where was my damn class?*

14

~~FIRST~~ WORST DAY

On the day of the interview, no one had told me my section or who would be my form tutor. The first teacher I saw, was an old lady with short hair, dressed in a sari, inside the grand library on my left side, I pushed aside the glass doors, and went inside. Before I could get to her and ask about who I should go to, I was told to step outside because I had a bag in my hand.

So, I quickly went outside to keep my bag. By the time I returned to the library which had shelves full of books in all languages and colors, it was too late because the teacher had already left the library. *But who cares? I needed to find someone else who'd help me.*

That's all!

I smiled and went outside, to pick up my bag and find someone who'd help me. I walked through the buzzing corridors and wondered, how did those kids have so much energy on a Monday morning? How can anyone have *that* much of energy on a Monday morning? *I mean, I was kind of dying already.*

I started to read each title on the doors of the rooms, as I walked ahead. The first one read 'Ms. Meera Aggarwal – Physics,' that seemed useless. The next one read 'Ms. Anvita Sharma – Mathematics,' again no use to me. The third one was on the door to a comparatively smaller room which was well lit. It read 'Ms. Om Prie Srivastava – MYP manager' and I figured that she was probably the best person to ask for help.

So, I knocked on the door and waited for her to answer. A faint voice replied from within "Come in darling." I stepped inside the room with boards filled with images of children and pages that seemed like notices for students and teachers.

Seated there was a mid-aged woman, dressed in a wine-colored sari, with salt and pepper hair and a face full of tension. I could tell from her expression that she was perhaps overloaded with work because she genuinely seemed like a nice person.

As I stood there clueless about my next move, she initiated the conversation by questioning me, "Good morning darling, are you a new student? how can I help you?" Since, she looked so welcoming and willing to help, I asked her who my form tutor was.

After I inquired, I was told to find a teacher whose name as I recall, was Ms. Sanskriti Arora. According to the coordinator, I would find Ms. Arora in "the quietest and most disciplined room, a room where the students would probably be meditating or were in deep thought. She has wavy light hair and a very fair complexion." She continued, "Just ask any kid, everyone knows Ms. Arora and she'll help you out."

The Burning Truth

Once she completed her sentence, she passed me a gigantic smile, and I took my cue from her and exited the room. As I stepped outside I felt relieved for a while, I thought to myself...*at least there's one-person willing to help.*

By now, just about every kid had disappeared into their classes. The only person who was outside, in front of the black colored lockers, was the boy who had embarrassed me in the bus. Helplessly, I chose to inquire from him about the whereabouts of Ms. Arora.

Surprisingly, the minute I started to advance towards him, he seemed a little startled, and on catching a glimpse of me, he opened the nearest locker and slid a rectangular box inside, which resembled a cigarette box. But I convinced myself that it was a calculator of some sort. After taking care of the rectangular box, he showcased almost all his teeth and smiled at me.

I finally asked him, "Hey, I just talked to umm... Ms. ... Oh! I forgot her name, basically, I talked to the coordinator or manager...and-"

He interrupted me and said, "Okay dude, you gotta hurry up, I have a class with Ms. Arora, and she hates students who are-"

"Oh! She's the teacher who I am trying to find." I enthusiastically told him.

He seemed a little paranoid, but maybe because he was getting late, he chose to not waste time on expressing his distress. My feet worked in parallel to him, following his lead. When we reached, I could see a teacher who seemed quite welcoming from the small window pane of the door. As soon as I entered the classroom, I could feel all eyes staring at me. However, the most piercing pair belonged to that teacher.

Her gaze was objecting, and it read, "Why are you interrupting our meditation session?" but instead she raised one of her eyebrow and said, "Good morning dear."

After wishing her well, I asked her, "Ma'am, I'm actually a new student and I am not aware which section am I supposed to go to... The umm...manager...told me to ask you."

"Oh sure, I will tell you. When you climb up the stairs, there's this large red pin board kept on the side, which has the details of the allocated sections of all the new students as well as directions..." Her lips suddenly stopped moving, and her face grew serious, "Didn't you come across the list on your way here?"

At this point, I couldn't tell if she was being sarcastic, rude, or simply asking a question. I convinced myself that probably it was the latter, swallowed all my anger and replied, "Actually ma'am I took the staircase that umm...comes up at the library, and I didn't catch sight of any board."

The girl who I had seen in the bus with the golden highlights, rose her hand and before she got the permission to speak, she pointed out, "Ms. Arora, I think she took the old staircase, so she missed the board." Although I think she was trying to help me, for some reason, I could see all students suddenly chuckling softly, looking at me. *What's new in that?*

After some discussion, Ms. Arora, finally told me where the Red Board is. Yes, she still hadn't told me my class, even though I could sense that a list was probably sitting right on her desktop. Nevertheless, I went to that daunting little red board, and found my misspelt name 'Saana' next to Form 9C and the name of the form tutor was mentioned as Ms. Rashmi Sehgal.

In some time, I finally reached the right class. The wooden door labelled '9C' lead to a class full of gigantic blue boards, covered by pages written in different languages, colorful drawings of weird things like unicorns and lots of group images. In the front of the class were three separate boards. The first one was a lot tinier than the other two, while the center one seemed a little odd, it had icons drawn all over the edges, and on the side, was a unique marker which was inkless. The last board was the one which seemed like a normal whiteboard.

When I had entered the class, I was greeted by a very thin lady with red cheeks, and short curly hair. For some reason, she seemed like a nice person, and there was a positive vibe coming from her. As soon as I got to her dark-brown wooden table, where she was seated in front of her laptop, dressed in a floral top and a blue trouser, she stood up and gave me a firm, yet gentle handshake coupled with a gigantic smile.

When she finally let go of my hand, I wheezed a little.

"Welcome to the family... Saana!

After I told her my name, and how it's pronounced, she realized that I had no place to sit, which is why I was still standing on her head. I saw that unlike my last school, where we all sat in groups, here, there were only two-seater wooden tables. Which meant, when Ms. Sehgal asked the class, "Who would like to scooch a little, so that Sana can sit with them?" *I knew I had trouble coming my way.*

I could feel the room get tense, and the heat rise. All eyes were suddenly staring at me again, as though I was lying on the operation table, with my body open, in front of a group of doctors who were all fighting with each other about who can hurt me more, and hence, who should go first.

After a minute, of no response from anyone, Ms. Sehgal finally got the cue that no one wanted to sit with 'me' the new girl, for some obvious reason. So, Ms. Sehgal asked a guy called Mohan, to allow me to sit next to him. But he too refused flat, saying, "Ma'am, I have a contagious sneezing problem, which may affect the new girl. So, I don't think…"

Seriously? He looked completely normal. At least make up a suitable excuse dude. Ms. Sehgal still agreed that "It can be very dangerous" and that she didn't want me sick just when the school has started.

Thus, she went ahead and asked another girl this time; someone whose name sounded like 'Jay – Yoon' but I was sure that it wasn't that. The girl was probably Korean, I thought.

Anyway, when she asked the girl with the straight dark brown hair, tiny thin eyes, and abnormally long legs, she replied in a blunt tone, "If I let her sit with me today, would this seating arrangement be permanent?" Ms. Sehgal seemed a little confused. After a moment, she responded saying, "Well, I think it's best if we make permanent seating arrangements. So…yes."

Once again, I was rejected by the Korean girl too.

By now, I could tell Ms. Sehgal was getting angry. Her lips were no more twisted on the edges. Her cheeks were suddenly tomato red, plumped with anger and she had put one hand on her hip as she walked from her table to the center of the class.

I had expected something good, something in my defense, because those little bastards had embarrassed me by not giving me a seat. She finally came to my rescue, and said, "Children, we are one society, one class, one family. That means we can't leave any member behind. So, please...someone...just let her sit. After all, doesn't the saying go, *no smurf left behind!*" She said all of this in the nicest way possible.

Not what I was expecting, not. at. all.

15

THE FIRE DRILL?

After Ms. Sehgal had made a fool of not only me but also herself, finally, the new girl from the bus, who was seated at the back of the class all this while, gave me a seat next to her. However, all the drama and the waiting had gone in vein because, as soon as I had hung my bag on the hook of the table, a loud bell rang, and suddenly, all students carelessly scurried out of the class, barely giving a damn about who they had hit or run over in the process.

Soon I realized that it was a fire alarm, so I quickly picked up my bag and decided to follow the crowd because I was unaware of the assembling spot. I followed them through the corridors, towards the library and down the staircase. For some odd reason, everyone seemed happy and I failed to understand why.

I mean there was a fire in the building! How the hell could anyone be laughing and giggling at this point?

Then I thought I cracked it. The reason why everyone was laughing and seemingly happy was because they were missing a lesson of probably Mathematics or something. This happened in our last school too. Every time we had a drill, everyone used to be so happy because we missed a lesson.

When we had finally reached the big field which I had seen on the day of my interview, I noticed it was only Grade 9 who was in the ground. Then I understood, this drill was only for students of my grade. Although that made it very obvious that it was a drill and not a real fire... but who am I to say anything?

We were all told to stand in queues according to our sections by a middle-aged man with a dark brown complexion and a bald head. He was wearing track pants along with a shining white t-shirt and muddy sport shoes.

There was a girl standing in front of me in the line who had red highlights and long tumbleweed hair along with a curvy body which she probably wanted me to notice...in a weird way. I gathered all my courage and patted on her shoulder gently.

She looked around and I suddenly started to blink my eyes so rapidly that it freaked me out itself. When I saw her face, I couldn't really see it. Because it was covered in excessive make up. Her eyelashes were covered in mascara and eyeliner, her cheeks seemed perfectly carved and highlighted while her lips were full of lipstick of the color of pomegranate seeds.

What in the world...was she? A supermodel or something?

After awing over her for about what seemed like infinity, I finally asked her, "So, is this fire drill only for us...as in our grade?" She replied with a perplexed expression, "A Fire drill?" For some reason, she said that loud enough ensuring that the entire grade, including the bald teacher, could hear her loud and clear.

"Wait a minute...did you think that this entire exercise was a fire drill?"

So, I figured that I was probably mistaken. I tried to process...this wasn't a fire drill. I replied, "No...not at all. Why would I think that!?" It turned out to be a little sarcastic, and she probably caught it. Frankly, let me admit, *I am not a good liar.*

"Alright guys listen up," she said as she gestured at everyone to form a group. "This new girl right here, thought this was a fire drill. Wait, so who do you think is the baldy right there?" She said pointing at the man in the track pants.

"Umm...I, uh...I don't know." By this point, I knew that I was getting nowhere by lying! I could feel the sweat run down my back and face. I had even felt my hands shiver and my eyes grow big. Thankfully, the track pants teacher came to my rescue, or so I thought.

He immediately told the group to split up and stand in lines. That's when I noticed the volley balls, the cricket bat and the basketball, all kept on the side of the field. And it suddenly hit me, *it was a fricking sports lesson!* For a second I was really happy because I had cracked the puzzle. Perhaps, that was the reason everyone rushed down, it seemed like they loved the sports lesson. That was the reason why we were all assembled in the field... to play some sport!

While I had been thinking all of this, a girl behind me shook my shoulder, as though trying to wake me up.

When I looked at her, she pointed at the teacher who was calling me and the girl who had earlier embarrassed me. I was delighted, there was finally someone who would take these bastards down. I rushed towards him with a smiling face while the other girl followed.

16

NATZI IS BACK

When we had finally reached the corner of the field where he was standing, I didn't really get very good vibes from him. He gave me a strange look. I remember him saying, "I don't understand. A new girl...create so much chaos, probably on her number one day. Not good, not good." Instead of listening to what he was saying, I was laughing within, *why do most sports teachers speak English like this?*

Since I had zoned out, when he asked me, "Are you hearing my words speaking?" I was clueless. Then I finally heard him say, "Look new girl, you are not allowed to make problem here, especially around with our star child."

Wait a minute...was this the same 'star' student who had embarrassed ME. This is not about me troubling her. What the hell? On what basis do the teachers even judge a student or punish them here? I just had to stand up for myself. This was totally unacceptable.

So, under the scorching Sun, with all students staring at both of us, I looked at him straight in the eye, and replied, "Sir... I don't understand. I am a new student, and

The Burning Truth

it was clearly a misinterpretation of the situation, since I thought it was a fire drill. As a matter of fact, I created no chaos until this girl drew all the attention towards us, without any adequate reason."

I thought that I had made myself clear. This wasn't my fault. But instead, I was told by the bald teacher, "First you calling me a baldy, I act to pretend to ignore you calling me that, because you is a new girl. But then, you trying to humiliate me on using big words and fancy English...will be no help. Understand?"

By now, I had given up on what had been happening. I had dropped the idea of standing up for myself and all that crap. I tried to lock my tears which were on the rim of my eyelids, waiting to drop. I apologized to him, "I am very sorry sir. This was all my fault."

"Yes, it indeed is. You is debarred from all sport lessons for next two weeks. Okay?"

"Yes sir."

Wow! talk about bad luck *and* bad teachers. I wiped away my tears and waited for him to lead the way and move towards all others who were exercising in lines. As soon as I started to move behind him, the other girl forcefully swirled me around to face her.

Her one eyebrow rose in a peculiar way, and her lips were giving me a nasty smile. "So...*new girl.* You thought you would use some crooked words and persuade sir that I, Natasha Goel, the *star student* of this school was at fault and not you?"

Without even giving me the time to comprehend what she was saying or answer, she started talking again. She put both her hands on her hips and continued speaking, "Well, if you did. You were wrong...very wrong. And trust me, by taking a stand for yourself, you didn't do a good thing. You would have to pay for this; sooner or later."

This whole episode had just blown me off. I stepped a little closer, looked at her with the sternest expression and stated, "So, you, whatever Goel are telling me that standing up for oneself is wrong? That you were not the one who tried to humiliate me in front of the entire grade? Because if that's what you're saying...trust *me*, it won't be good."

I had sensed a cat fight coming my way, but by that point, I was just so done for the day, starting with the embarrassing bus ride followed by the hunt to find my class. Then my attempt at finding a seat, then all of this. Finally, I decided to just go with it.

If this had been a comical action story, I would've said that I could clearly see the red flames and steam come out of her ears, but it actually wasn't. Anyway, she was pretty angry and to show her disgust she almost spat as she declared, "The war is on, you *bitch.*"

I too was unstoppable at that moment and was clearly unsure of what my mouth was blabbering and so, I told her, "Yes, *it is on.*"

17

THE (UN) WILLING VOLUNTEER

A few minutes after Natasha was gone, I contemplated a little, and realized that me not apologizing to her and instead accepting her war invitation wasn't a very wise decision. My mind diverted as I started thinking about what she'd probably do to me, in fact, I thought of what is the worst thing she could do to me.

I thought of putting ice down their shirt during mathematics. Or, I could chop and rip apart their swimming costumes when they are in the pool. Another one could be, stealing away all their stationery during examination. And the worst that of all, making a fake complain against them with Gauri Ma'am, our deadly teacher at FPS who gave me goosebumps every time we talked.

In my case, all of them seemed possible, and they were all very deadly apart from the last one since it doesn't match all the criteria. Nevertheless, in short, I was scared.

Later, after sports, or what they call P.H.E., we all headed upstairs, back to our class. Where, Ms. Sehgal again courteously accepted the opportunity to embarrass me. All of us, took our spots. Once again, I went and sat next to the sweet Shimla girl from the bus. As soon as we started to talk, and for the first time, someone showed some sympathy towards me. She told me that she was proud that I stood up for myself against the Natasha kid.

Soon after, I had started listening to what Ms. Sehgal was saying, I figured she was talking about Me. Again. But why? I became aware that she was on the hunt of trying to assign me a 'buddy' who was apparently supposed to help me in understanding the school and its people. I very desperately needed one, considering my current situation.

Once more, she started by asking everyone, "Who would like to volunteer for being Sana's buddy?" and in no time, she was begging for someone to become my buddy. I was honestly really disturbed by this. But then, out of the blue, a guy stood up and said, "Ms. Sehgal, can I be her buddy?"

This volunteer had chestnut colored short hair and his eyes were full of pride. He was merely an inch or two taller than me and his physique resembled Aman. This was probably the reason I did not want to look at him, after all, I couldn't really stand the idea of talking to Aman again.

But then, I didn't really have a choice.

Once the class was dismissed, I walked towards him to ask why did he, of all people, decide to volunteer as a buddy for me. When I did, he hesitated before replying, "Umm... I don't know, just like that I guess..."

"Well, regardless of what the reason may be... I am glad you opted to help me out, I was kinda lost here. And nothing good has really happened just yet."

His face grew serious as if he wanted to know more, so I told him all about the worst day ever. As soon as I started to talk about the Natasha incident, his face grew serious, and I saw his eye twitch. He didn't say a word about her, in my defense.

I wondered why?

18

-TRUTH-

That day, when I returned home, I knew that Mumma was expecting a detailed report and an account of my first day at Avenues International. But how could I possibly tell her, that that day was undoubtedly the worst day of my life?

Plus, by temperament, she was not even very resilient to traumatic incidents. That was made very clear in the fall of 2016, when I had told her about how *I* slipped on a banana peel and ended up falling. She was so traumatized by that petty incident, that we had to rush *her* to the hospital immediately.

That is why, I came up with the most enjoyable and positive story of my first day at Avenues. The story was something like this:

"The day started off well. In the bus, I found another new girl who was equally nervous and we got the opportunity to talk about each other's former schools and life. Next, as soon as I climbed the stairs, I saw the list on a red board which stated that I am in grade 9C. Once I got to the class, Ms. Sehgal (the nicest teacher ever) allotted me a seat right in the front of the

class, next to a very nice girl who was later also willing to be my buddy. Apart from the studies, we also had the PE lesson, where we all got to play any game of our choice. All in all, it was a wonderful day."

I consoled myself by thinking that she was at least happy, because as soon as I told her this, she started to cry with tears of joy. She then wrapped her hands around me in a manner that almost took my breath away, and whispered in my ear, "I am so happy, that you are happy." When she pulled away, in a deep voice she said, "you can't imagine how worried I was…about this day going wrong for you. I prayed for you the entire day. I knew it would be all good. I am so happy for you, beta."

I knew that I couldn't tell her the truth and so I didn't. Instead, I smiled at her and went back to my room. I thought to myself, even though I had lied, I knew it was for the better of Mumma. And so, I calmed myself with that and went to the washroom.

After changing, I chose to check WhatsApp and with a ray of hope to connect again, tried to text Ria, since she still hadn't replied to my text from the other night. And that's when I realized, she had blocked me on WhatsApp!

Or maybe…she has just removed her profile picture. Or, she has perhaps deactivated her account. I mean, she often did that when her mom confiscated her phone. So, it was possible. I shouldn't freak out. I'll just try contacting her through some other mode, like Instagram. Or Snapchat. Or Facebook. Or even WeChat. I mean, I am sure she'll reply soon. There are endless reasons for her to not reply!

I didn't give up. I decided that I would text her on other social media accounts the following day.

I was scrolling through my Facebook feed when I decided to add my school change to my profile, thinking it might give a hint to Ria and all others who might be wondering where have I disappeared to. As soon as I added 'Avenues International School' to my profile, a list of friend suggestions came up under my notifications.

I started to browse them one at a time. The first one was 'Gamini Khanna.' According to her profile she was living at The Magnolias, *high profile alert!* Her profile picture suggested she had a really cute Papillion and her mother was some sort of model because she was only visible in bikinis and super-hot dresses. She had 723 friends, which obviously meant she was popular. However, she for some reason had not posted a single picture of herself.

Self-conscious much?

The next person who appeared under suggestions was incidentally Natasha Goel, the girl who wanted to ruin my already ruined life. Her profile was an accurate depiction of who she seemed like to me.

A girl wearing a black dress which barely covered her thighs, along with a cute silver purse hung on her shoulder; was seated on the rim of a window along with a cigarette stuck to her mouth in her profile picture. She seemed more beautiful than how she looked at school. It seemed as though the cigarette somehow magically increased her coolness level.

She had a whopping 1083 friends on her Facebook profile and I couldn't help but think, *how can I compete against her?*

As I scrolled through her profile, one of her posts showed her dressed in a black leather jacket along with super tight and long black boots and a heavy-duty helmet which fitted her head just like a crown. Her excess, beautiful hair blew with the wind as she rode a Harley Davidson. *Even though she was barely 15 I'm guessing.* And she had got about 858 likes for that picture. *How did she even get them?*

The next profile that popped up under suggestions from Natasha was the guy from the bus. Now, I learnt that his name was Ansh Roy who lived somewhere in Malibu Towne.

He was definitely a popular kid because his Fb Bio literally said, "I'm admired at Avenues." Which although does sound crazy and stupid, but did ring a bell. The next thing that caught my eye on his wall was his cover photo that was of him with a bunch of kids who didn't really seem like kids. They were about twelve of them, all sitting by some water body, which was probably a pool because it had under water lights with their legs dipped in water.

They were posing with their hands wrapped around one another and this guy had a weird goofy smile on his face. He sat there in a black button up shirt which wasn't really buttoned up, along with a pair of shorts. Onto his right was a girl who seemed like a duplicate version of Natasha, and talking of the devil, next to the duplicate, sitting there was Natasha with a cigarette stuck in her mouth, in a bright red short dress which probably had some drink like white wine poured all over it, along with a couple of other girls.

Onto his left side were a group of boys who were wearing similar shirts and in some cases, no shirts. Honestly, they didn't even look that hot or anything. But I was still jealous, and it took me a little while to realize this, but I was probably jealous of their friendship, their bond and what they had, but I didn't.

That night, I decided to sleep with only one thought in mind: Tomorrow will be better.

19

THE NOTE

I looked at my watch, which showed 1:23. I had precisely seven minutes to go and find my school bag before the bell rang for Spanish, a lesson which I couldn't be late for, as my teacher for Spanish was Ms. Sanskriti Arora, the form tutor of 9D, also known as the scariest and strictest teacher at Avenues International, although I must say I've heard that without her...nothing gets done here.

So, without giving it much of a thought, I raced from the Dining Hall to tell Ms. Sehgal about someone stealing my bag.

I was just around the corner and I could clearly see 9C when I banged into our Principal almost flipping her onto the floor.

"What are you up to Sana!" She yelled at me, lying on the floor.

I stepped towards her in an attempt to pick her up from the floor. I stretched my hand to offer her support, and she firmly grasped it. It felt she barely took my help and was instead simply trying to squash my hand to teach me a lesson. As soon as she rose, she started talking, "I don't understand. What were you doing, running at such a fast speed, *in the corridors?* Look Sana, we value your talent as an athlete, but that is only to be exhibited in the field. Not inside the school. I hope I've made myself clear?"

I lowered my head and in a voice, that was almost inaudible I replied, "Yes ma'am. My apologies."

She still seemed unconvinced but I decided to leave, because according to my watch, I had precisely 60 seconds left to go to Ms. Sehgal. I rushed into the class to tell her, but to make my already bad day, even worse, as I banged open the door, and instead of the happy-going Ms. Sehgal sitting on the chair, I found almost all MYP teachers seated in the room.

Yep. All of them.

All my teachers got the sight of my sweaty and literally messy side, that day. All my hair was out of the pony tail, and scattered on my face. My eyes were popping out due to all the running and accidents. My hands were trembling and I had no words left for explaining my situation.

The teachers who were now standing with their books in their hands looked at me with the eyes of an examiner. I felt as though I was Draupadi who's being stripped in front of the entire middle school staff. The only difference? I had no savior who would come and save me from all these teachers whose expression told that they had multiple questions about me running in their minds such as –

why is she panting like a dog? Why and how did she just barge into the room like that? Why does she look like she just ran a marathon? What is wrong with this new girl? Is she abnormal or something?

I decided to simply not look at any of them, or make any sort of eye contact. Instead, I walked straight towards Ms. Sehgal and screamed, "They stole my bag!" She seemed as terrified as just about every teacher in that room. Her forehead had innumerable tension lines and her cheeks went almost pale.

She immediately stood up and directed me to go outside and talk. As we exited the room, I could hear all the teachers whisper and chatter like little kids about me. *Why was this happening?*

Once we were outside in the corridor, Ms. Sehgal looked at me, waiting for an explanation. Even though according to my watch the Spanish lesson had already begun, I tried to calm myself down, and tell her the entire sequence of events.

"Ma'am to begin with, I carry my bag to dining hall because I didn't know which place to keep it. So, I was eating...and my bag...it was kept on the side. You know the place from where we enter and there's a wall on the side, there. And I was eating so I couldn't see who took my bag... but when I came back to pick my bag, it wasn't there!"

She looked at me as if she was really concerned, not angry. And said, "Look Sana darling, at Avenues friends do keep stealing bags of one another. I mean, they aren't stealing, it's just a prank so–"

"But ma'am I have *no friends!* So, this can't be the reason or explanation!"

"Beta I am not sure how I can help you with this. You should probably go to the lost and found section and see if your bag has reached there. Otherwise...just wait."

Just wait? This was my bag that we were talking about. It has all my books and notebooks. It had just about every possible thing that is valuable for my academic journey at Avenues International. And she's telling me to *just wait?*

Also, how could anyone be so calm when something like this happens? I actually admired her for this quality.

When I entered the Spanish class twenty-one minutes late, with no excuse slip and no books or notebooks, it was a sad scene for me. Ms. Arora screamed almost so loud that it could have possibly been heard from three blocks away. She then gave me a time out and her exact words were, "Never, and by Never, I mean *never*, enter my class *late and without* a notebook. Now get out of my sight!"

On the bright side, after searching the entire school, visiting the bookshop at least one thousand times, and asking every student possible if they had seen my rose-printed, pink colored bag, I finally found it by the end of the day.

It was kept in the cubicle of the girl's washroom. At that moment, I realized what true happiness felt like. Then I thought, *when did I come to the washroom with my bag?* And I realized, I didn't. But I was just happy that I finally found my bag.

The Burning Truth

Later when I reached home, I re-processed everything that had happened with me on my sixth day at Avenues International School. Although this event was tragic, I was suddenly smiling, because I recalled that from next week onwards, I could start swimming with everyone else, because I would no longer be debarred due to that sassy little bitch, Natasha.

That's when it hit me. Maybe this entire 'losing school bag thing' was also her idea. I immediately started to ransack my bag throwing things out one after the other, when I came across a tiny little fluorescent yellow note that was neatly folded. As I opened it, it read,

"Hey Sana,

Hoping you enjoyed today. Many more such days to come...

Love, Natz."

I knew it was her! What is wrong with her? She stole my bag and got it hidden just for that petty issue that happened during sports... I couldn't believe that she damaged my newly born reputation with all my teachers and the principal... Plus, my academics went for a toss, and truth be told, I had a really bad day. *Why is she doing this? What will she do next?*

20

THE RACE I ACED

There were just two days left for me to complete my first two weeks at Avenues International School, and I couldn't be happier. After all, one of the major reasons that persuaded me to come to this school was swimming. Even though Aman ditched me as a boyfriend and as a swimming coach, I was still determined to learn, and something from within told me that my turn to win medals would come soon.

Thinking this, I went with my head up high to school that day. The bus ride was still dreadful. The only bright moment in that twenty-minute ride was when Ansh came aboard and passed me a smile as well as every now and then we exchanged a word or two. He often inquired from me if I was doing fine at school, and if I had any problem.

I obviously told him that *everything is great.* From his Facebook profile, I remembered that my buddy was friends with Ansh. So, I mentioned him whenever possible, just to show that I too had some connections. And even though Ansh seemingly didn't have the best reputation as a stellar academic student, he did seem like a nice kid to me.

When we reached school, I headed straight up to my class. Our first lesson was Economics. I quickly dropped my attendance with Ms. Sehgal and rushed to Mr. Khanna, our Eco Teacher. He was a thirty-something and his trademark was his Nehru Style jacket, whose buttons barely met on his rotund tummy.

I was the first one to enter the class and take a seat. As soon as I did, Mr. Khanna looked at me and gave me a stupendous smile. I really liked him as a teacher, since he was always so lively and chirpy. Perhaps, he was the only reason I ever developed interest in the subject.

That reminded me, it was the day we got our first unit test grades, and it was a big day indeed. So, this smile was definitely a good sign for me. Or maybe, it was just a consoling smile because I have failed the test.

I closed my eyes, joined my hands and prayed, *oh God, I hope it isn't the latter.* After everything that had happened in the past *almost* two weeks, I needed good grades. These grades were my only hope, for now at least. On opening my eyes, I saw that some other kids had also arrived for the class.

Mr. Khanna finally rose from his chair and looked at all of us with a sympathetic expression. His eyes became small and narrow, his eyebrows twitched, and a gentle smile appeared on his face. The lines on his face had disappeared. I knew what was coming wasn't good. *I failed. I know I failed, no point in hearing him out.*

"Students, as you would all recall, we recently had our unit test on Supply and Demand Curves. In my hand, are your marked papers. My overall feedback is that... Well, I'm disappointed."

I just knew it. I had to fail, didn't I? Why do this to me God, why?

Since I had obviously zoned out, thinking about the misery of my life, I suddenly realized, that almost every child in the class was looking at me as though *I* have committed a crime. That's when Dev, my only 'friend' whispered in my ear, "You got the highest marks Sana."

I almost shouted in a creaky voice, "I got the highest marks?" He nodded in a way which I could tell that he was disappointed. That's when I realized, everyone staring towards me was sad and miserable, because they hadn't done as well as me in their assessment.

At last, *something good* had happened with me, finally.

That day, I walked out of the class with my head up high with pride. That feeling lasted barely a minute because before I could go any further, Natasha and her friends had created a human wall around me, restricting me from going any further.

I put on my calmest face, trying not to rub off my happiness in her face, because I knew that would simply piss her off. She crossed her hands and stood with her legs apart, just like a gangster, who's about to get me beaten up.

"Hey Natasha." I called out.

"Sana just because you topped in a subject like Economics doesn't really mean that you've won this race."

The Burning Truth

"What race? And how in the world did you *already* get to know about my grades?"

"A. The race between you and I, in which *I* am obviously winning. And B. I have my sources, I know *everything*."

"Look, you say you know everything, but what you don't know is that this isn't a race."

"Oh honey, it surely is. And let me tell you a little secret, the next time you do well in *any* assessment, in an attempt to rub it in my face, it won't be good." She said sarcastically, in a high pitch.

Until this point, I was calm and minding my own business. But this just blew me off, how can *she* tell *me* to do something?

"Wait, so you're telling me...that I *need* to do badly in my bands, because you are insecure about you getting lesser grades than me?"

"Did *you* just say that I am insecure because of you?"

WHAT WAS WRONG WITH ME? Why do I just keep bringing on more trouble for myself every damn time. I thought, I must apologize immediately, but thankfully that wasn't required because the other new Shimla Girl who I had met on the bus came to my rescue. *Turned out that this school did have some good people after all!*

Before Natasha could get a chance to reply back, Mr. Khanna intervened and cooled off the matter.

That was a close escape...thank God!

21

FIRST DAY AT SWIMMING

As we all rushed down the staircase, our slippers flipping and clapping with each step on the staircase, the only thing I could think about was the fact that those torturous two weeks were finally over. As I took a step into the swimming arena, I could feel my stomach turn upside down. My hands were getting cold and so was my face.

Inside the four walls of that area, was a gigantic half Olympic size swimming pool. As I stepped inside, I could feel the smell of the pool, which was probably due to the excessive chloramines; travel through my nose and into my body, giving me a long-awaited tingling feeling. The lightly cold, wet and moist floor around the pool touched my feet. The swooshing sound of the water flow through the side canals topped it all. And at last, I had caught sight of the crystal-clear water, waving at me, wanting me to dive in.

"So, how long time is you planning to stand here and watch at the pool Ms...umm Sana?"

My thoughts were interrupted by the same teacher who had debarred me from PE for two whole weeks.

The Burning Truth

At that minute, I felt like punching his stupid face and knocking his head down to the floor, but I knew that if I wanted to learn swimming, then I had to build a good reputation with him.

I put all my anger aside and looked at him straight in the eye. "Not another minute sir, because I am only here to work towards my dream which is to excel in swimming, and fantasizing about it won't help. Please allow me Sir, to go and change."

He seemed staggered down to the soul. He was definitely not expecting something like this to come from the *new girl who caused a chaos on her first day.* He smiled at me, and nodded a little. And I knew, *nothing could stop me from excelling in this, nothing but me.*

After changing into my swimwear, as I walked towards the swimming pool, following a group of other girls, who seemed least interested in including me to their group, I promised to myself, I would not let any sort of enemy or fight get into this and ruin it.

The funniest part about this whole exhilaration I felt for swimming was, I had barely ever swum before. When I did, it was just for fun, splashing around the pool. I knew the basic strokes, but I wasn't any expert, and I never thought of becoming one, until I saw Aman take part in the swimming competition that day. And as I said before, I too wanted to feel the adrenaline rush, through my body. I too wanted to win like him. And now, I undoubtedly wanted to be someone better than him in this sport.

The class started with the same bald teacher introducing himself as we sat in the corner of the arena in clusters, I just sat towards the back of the girls group. He started by saying, "For new comers, is this introduction. I is called Mr. Aryan Jain. And I say only one thing, if you work hard with I, we can take you to national and even international level. Also, my one rule is that never laugh on my English. I sometimes talk in Hindi too, because I is a sports teacher, not English. Okay?"

We all mumbled yes and some of us nodded too. He then continued, "Ms. Geetika Yadav is join me now and talk about herself."

The first time I saw Ms. Yadav, I finally saw hope. After all, having the facility of a heated half Olympic size pool was different, but having someone to teach how to swim in it, was a different thing altogether. And honestly, Mr. Jain did not seem like a person who could teach me how to swim, probably Ms. Yadav would. She was way too fit for an average Indian woman, and her body posture and clothing told she was a real athlete.

She put her hands on her waist and said, "I am your swimming instructor, assisting Mr. Jain. Like him, I too have one rule, *swim* and keep swimming, until you get it right. And that's it. Now go, and follow my rule."

I think for a second no one really got what she was saying. But then I figured it, she wanted us to get up from the floor, stop wasting time, and just swim. So, I quietly stood up, while others looked up at me. Then I walked towards the swimming pool and jumped in. For some odd reason, I could feel a sense of pride as I did so, probably because I was the only one who got what she was saying.

In about two minutes, everyone was inside the pool. We were all full of excitement, and my level...was the highest. I was extremely happy, and it felt nice to be happy every once in a while.

Ms. Yadav came stomping towards us, with a stopwatch in hand. She paused for a second, and then loudly told us, "We'll follow our regular routine all right? First warm up, then main set and then recovery. Any questions?"

Oh boy, I had so many words to understand. What is a set? Like, I've done it in Mathematics, it's about circles and numbers. But... I don't know what it has to do with swimming. Plus, what exactly are we expected to do in warm up? Also, is it like we'd be dead or something, that we'd need recovery? It felt like she was speaking an alien language.

I tapped my buddy's shoulder and asked him, "What exactly do all those words, she just said mean?"

I guess, he was kind of pissed. But then, he looked at me with what I'd call pity, and replied, "Just follow my lead."

And so, I did.

22

SWIMMING AND SMOKING

That one hour of swimming was probably the longest 3600 seconds of my life. As Ms. Yadav had said, we started with warm up, wherein she made me do exercises (I had never heard of before!). The first one was something called a forward lunge, which we were apparently supposed to do about a hundred times. *No big deal for a person who hardly ever gets out of the house or even goes for a walk.*

Next, she told us to do a 90–90 stretch, and although it may sound funny, trust me, it wasn't nearly as fun to do it. And before I could make my way to sixty 90–90 stretches, I was done. So, I started to cheat a little, but it's fine, *because I was only trying to save myself from dying.*

Following this, we did something known as... Standing Back Flexion/Extension and Lateral Extension. But I couldn't take it anymore. It was too much for me, and so, before I could stop it from happening, I fell onto the floor with a thud, onto my elbows *thankfully.*

I don't precisely remember what exactly happened after that, but I know that I hadn't been gone long.

The Burning Truth

Because when I woke up, I was not in an infirmary. I was not at home. I was still in the swimming arena. And I was surrounded by students who were looking down at me like I'm a lab rat. Standing in the center of all of them was Ms. Yadav.

Someone splashed some chemically, swimming pool water on my face, and Ms. Yadav shouted, "C'mon Sana! This was barely anything! Get back on your feet!"

My eyes found the clock and I realized, there were still 40 minutes left for the class to end. *How is this not over yet?*

I attempted to stand up, and looked at her and apologized. She didn't say anything to my face, but as she walked away with the other kids following her, I heard her say under her breath, "*Sick new kids.*"

The only good thing about me fainting was, that when I woke up, we were done with the warm up session. At least that's what I thought before I heard the commanding voice of Ms. Yadav instruct, "Time for sprints people. Get into the water!"

It went *on and on and on and on and on and on and on.* Just like a never-ending cycle, and then came the recovery time. The golden five minutes that we were given to rest and recover. And now it did make sense, because I *did almost die* and so yes, we *did need this* recovery time!

The bell rang, and I had a weird sense of satisfaction. It felt like I had survived the battlefield, a war. But what confused me was that I wanted more of it. I wanted to go there again, and take on whatever came my way. Even though it almost killed me, it gave me a thrill - a different type of fulfillment.

It was so much like trying the first cigarette. It has the power of ruining you, but after you get through the first one, it's like you've survived an inner war between your mind and your body. And once you try the first one, you always want more, and more.

My deep thoughts were interrupted by the loud whistle of Ms. Yadav, instructing us to get out of the pool.

As I stepped out of the water, climbing up the stairs, I could feel my swimming costume hug my body tight. I could tell that my hair was wet, and my goggles were full of water. And my soul, was complete. I wanted more and more of it.

And for reasons unknown, I felt empowered.

When I returned from the changing room, I waited a while for the other girls to come out. They obviously barely gave a damn about my existence, but I didn't want to climb three flights of stairs all by myself, alone.

While I sat there waiting on the wooden benches placed outside the changing rooms, I saw Ms. Yadav and Mr. Jain approach me. I stood up from the bench and looked straight at them. *Why were they coming towards me? Were they coming towards me? Or were they headed towards the door behind me? Was this about me fainting? What happened for God's sake? A multitude of questions came to my mind.*

Mr. Jain stood opposite me, standing next to him was Ms. Yadav. He gave me an expression that wasn't very easy to comprehend and said, "Ms. Yadav told me about what is happened today."

So, this is about me fainting. What do you expect from someone who hasn't ever even done a single set of squats in her entire life, and suddenly she has to do all these crazy things?

I looked down and said, "My apologies sir."

Ms. Yadav spoke in a stern voice, "What are you apologizing about? You fainting?"

Now I was clueless. "Yes... Ms. Yadav."

That was the first time I saw Ms. Yadav smile. Her cheeks suddenly seemed full, and her eyes swooped low, she looked at me in the eye and said, "Look Although it's too early to tell, I feel that you have a natural knack for swimming. And with some help, you can perfect your strokes and increase your stamina too."

I had no clue from where and how she had drawn this conclusion.

She continued, "What we are saying is...that you might want to consider applying for district level swimming competition, which is in about three months from now. But...the registration closes soon."

District level? They think I am ready for that? Isn't it too early for them to decide?

Mr. Jain pitched in, "We are not saying you is ready. But we feel you is capable."

"So, if you're interested..."

I was full of glee and so I almost squeaked, "Of course I am interested!"

She put her hands in her pockets and with a satisfied face, she said, "Alright then, we'll send you the details soon."

It was all like a dream coming true.

23

THE REVELATION

As I waited there on my front door, I imagined telling Mumma all about my terrific swimming story and how she'd react. When the helper opened the door, I was a little surprised. Nevertheless, I threw my bag aside and ran up to her room. Sitting inside was Mumma in a corner, with a book in hand.

"Mumma?"

"Hello Sana beta. You're back?"

I ran to her and hugged her tight. When I let go of her, she looked at me and raised an eyebrow the way she did whenever she was puzzled and happy at the same time. "So, what do I owe for this sudden love and happiness of my daughter to?"

"Swimming Mumma!"

"*Swimming?*" She asked in a surprised tone.

Before I knew it, I began to rant.

"Yes! I haven't told you this, but umm... I kind of like swimming. I mean, I know it may seem sudden, but I had been fantasizing about it since forever. And now, today... when I finally got to swim, it was amazing."

"Finally?"

"Wait. I'm not done yet Mumma. This is just the beginning. Today, something good actually happened with me. All this while, I had been thinking, that Avenues is bad luck. Because...you know... But today, the best thing happened."

"Look I'm losing you. What do you mean by bad luck?"

I wasn't really listening to whatever she said. I continued to go on, "Today, Ms. Yadav, my swimming instructor...she said, *I was capable of going* for district level swimming! Can you imagine that?"

She suddenly stood up from her chair, and covered my mouth with her hand. "Stop Sana. What are you saying, I don't understand!"

She didn't seem as happy as I expected her to look, instead, she seemed rather concerned and paranoid.

I forcefully removed her hand from my mouth and shouted "I don't understand you Mumma. How can you not be happy about this?"

She then pulled me down and made me sit next to her on the bed. She held my hands and said, "Beta I'm very happy about the whole district level thing...but what did you just say about how this was the first good thing that happened...I mean, you said that your first day was amazing *right?*"

I then realized what damage I had caused. While I was ranting, I spilled the beans.

A secret I had been trying to hide for so long had come out. I didn't want her to know about my miserable life at Avenues. How can I just blurt out something as crucial as this? *What is wrong with me?* More importantly, how should I tell her the truth?

I hesitated a little, but then I knew that it's pointless keeping it within anymore. "I don't know how to put this...but I didn't tell you because I knew it would break you from within. You put me in this school with so much of hope and aspirations. But it feels like...for some odd reason, ever since I've stepped into that building, nothing good has ever happened with me! Until today...that is."

Her breath was getting uneven and her hands had started to shake. I told her to sit back on the bed, while I fetched her some water. I waited over there, for her to relax. Because, I knew she was in too much of pressure.

With wrinkles on her forehead, and squinted eyes, she stammered, "So...what...umm...what are the...b-bad things that happened?"

It was too late to hide anything anymore, so I simply came clean. I told her about the entire fight with Natasha and how she had been challenging me, and troubling me ever since. I told her about how everyone had their own groups, and no one wanted me to be a part of theirs. I even told her about how my real first day actually went off.

And the funny part was, that I was expecting to console my mother, because I knew she couldn't take so much. But instead, by the end of my narration, I was lying in her bed, with my head in her lap, and she was running her fingers through my hair. Her pajamas had become cold and wet because of the rivers flowing through my eyes.

I just couldn't take it anymore.

I had no friends as well as no support. I constantly felt like an intruder. And I knew that I didn't fit in. As I thought of all of these things, I continued howling and crying. It felt like, all those feelings that I hadn't confessed to someone in so long, they were all finally coming out, and I couldn't suppress them anymore. They just poured out one after the other, and I had no control over myself.

I just wanted to tell Mumma everything, and so I did. Our quick five-minute conversation took me around two hours to complete. And that day, I realized, telling someone does help. Because, by the end of our conversation, I felt so much lighter from within. It felt like I had been carrying these heavy stones on my back and shoulder for so long, on an endless road in the desert. Right at the point when I had lost all hope and I was about to collapse with all that burden on myself, comes someone out from the dark, to help me with my burden.

It was a wonderful feeling.

After I finished telling her just about everything, she told me this.

"Look Sana, you don't always get what you want, or what you deserve. Sometimes you've got to fight for it. So, I'm telling you, it's time to put on those boxing gloves, and get ready for the match. And let me warn you, your opponent will always seem stronger, and mightier, but the truth is, you are as strong as you think you are. So,

The Burning Truth

think positive and don't give up. Also, always remember, I'll be there for you and I know that you'll get through this."

I smiled at her and told her how much this meant to me. Then, came the difficult part. Making her promise, not to tell Papa. When she remained unconvinced and her decision seemed final, I had to give her life-threatening arguments and she couldn't say no to them. *They always work!*

I hadn't felt so light and happy in a long while. I was about to leave the room, when Mumma called out for me.

"Beta, there's a mail from the school... I think it's about your swimming thing."

The details about the competition had arrived!

24

THE COMPETITION!

I raced to Mumma, and hopped onto her bed. Anxiously waiting for her to open and download the E-mail, I sat there anticipating what all could possibly be written in there. It seemed like she was on-purpose taking longer to open the Email, just to build up my excitement, but instead, it turned out, that the internet was slow.

When it finally opened, Mumma read it out to me.

Dear Parents,

It's an honor for the swimming federation at Avenues International School to announce that your ward, Sana Sharma is encouraged to participate in the swimming trials for Haryana District Level championship. This information is to share to the respective parents, so you are requested to complete the preliminary registration process, please refer to the following guide and fill it at the earliest.

Guide: Swimming Instruction
Name of the swimmer:
Name of the event:

Number of events:

Name of the Parents:

Father Name:

Mother Name:

Parents Phone Number:

Date of the selection Trials: Tomorrow

Venue of the selection Trials: Avenues International

Timings of registration: 7 am to 1 pm

Number of session per day:

- *Session 1–5 am to 8 am*
- *Session 2–10am to 12 pm*
- *Session 3–5 pm to 8 pm.*

Parent's Permission: Yes/No

Swimmer's Permission: Yes/No

Date of submission on or Before: 7th March, 2017

Kindly send your consensus on or before the prescribe date on the guide.

Best Regards,
The Swimming Federation
Avenues International School, Gurgaon

I looked at Mumma and we both shared the same, scared and confused look. That was perhaps the first time, I was unsure and uncertain about my capabilities. *Was I apt for these districts?*

I told Mumma that I needed some time to think, even though Ms. Yadav wanted me to reply soon. I mean, how can anyone expect someone to take such a big decision in a matter of seconds? So, I went back to my room, took off my clothes, and got into my thinking cabin, aka the shower.

I've always considered the shower as a sacred space where there is no one to disturb my thought process (except when Mumma comes and bangs on the door and threatens me to come out or else she would come in). It is a place where I have pondered and made many of my life decisions.

After turning on the shower, I started to contemplate about the mail.

I took out a yellow pad *in my mind,* and started to jot down the pros and cons for accepting this opportunity.

In my head, it looked somewhat like this:

Pros	Cons
I've always wanted to swim	I'd have to prioritize
It's like a wild card entry straight to districts	I have no stamina, (*I fricking fainted the other day*)
I'd get to prove myself in at least one field, where Natasha can't stop me	I'll need to work harder than others to catch up, and to get better

The last pros factor was all that I needed to convince myself that I need to apply for district level swimming championship. So, I quickly turned off the shower, put on a towel and rushed to Mumma's room.

When I charged into her room, she was a little (*understatement*) surprised.

"What...what happened Sana?"

"I've decided."

"That?"

"I'll do it."

"That's umm...great!"

"Well, I know I'll have to work really hard. But, as long as you believe and support me, I'll be fine."

"Of course, we are there for you beta. I'll just revert back to the mail. Till then, why don't you go and put on some clothes?"

I beamed with happiness and went away.

Since it was Friday, I had two days to prepare before my practice test that was to be held on Monday.

That evening itself, I set out on my first, official, swimming practice. We had a fairly gigantic pool in our society itself, so I decided, might as well go there and practice. Hence, I packed up my Kipling bag which was filled with a swimming costume, goggles, cap and towel.

We had two pools, out of which one was of no use, because most of the time, it was either crowded with oldies who had all the time in the world to relax, or little children who had no clue about time.

By the time I reached, it was rather dark and breezy. And so, the pool was lit with underwater lights. Those were one thing I loved about a pool. They made all the tiny little dust particles, which in other cases are invisible to the naked eye, seem like sparkle or glitter which is just fluttering in the water.

They made the water glow, and everything that glows looks beautiful, doesn't it?

I quickly changed into my swim wear and jumped into the pool. As soon as the cold, glittery water touched my skin, I realized that I forgot to warm up. So, I found my way out of the pool, and decided to do some 'easy' stretches.

A cold breeze blew, and all the leaves on the palm trees that surrounded the pool area, blew too. I felt a chill run down my spine, because I was still covered in water, and the breeze just made it worse. Thus, I quickly decided to jump back into the water to save myself from catching a cold.

Whenever I swam before, it was for pleasure. I'd perhaps take a few laps, some Insta-worthy pics, and then come out of the pool. But that evening, I remembered that I had no stamina and since now I knew that, I needed to work on it.

It was the first time in history that I did five laps back to back. I did all the strokes I knew: Breast, Freestyle, and Back. I felt satisfied when I was finished, the only problem? I knew that they wouldn't give me about a minute to relax after every lap.

But then, no one becomes a great swimmer in one day, right?

The next morning, I woke up at around six am When I walked out of my room at around 6: 30, I saw Mumma working on her laptop. Her face accurately said, *why is MY daughter out of her room at six-thirty in the morning on a Saturday?*

To clear her doubts, I told her that I am going to practice my strokes at the society swimming pool. I could tell she was astonished. But, when she walked up to me and checked if I had fever, I was left astonished.

"What are you doing Mumma?" I asked bluntly.

"What do you think I'm doing? I am obviously checking if you are alright, because if it is you, Sana Sharma, then I know that you can't be up so early."

"Well, I am. And you would see this happening very often. So be prepared. After all, if I've made a decision, then, I've got to work for it too, am I right?"

She seemed rather unconvinced but perhaps chose to go with the flow, "Uhhh... Yes, yes, sure."

I went to the kitchen, took out a Paper boat Aamras from the fridge and headed out of the main door. "Now you don't need to think about me staying hungry, all right?"

She chuckled a little and said, "You know me so well. Now go!"

I went for a swim at least six or seven times that weekend, and my mind said, "There's nothing more, that you can possibly do!" My heart clearly stated, "Something's missing." The night before my test, I barely slept, trying to fight the battle between my mind and my heart. But at the end of it, even though I convinced myself that I was ready, I could sense *something bad was about to happen.*

25

THE CHASE BEGINS

"I know you have it! I can see it!" I shouted as I ran across the corridor following a guy who I didn't exactly recognize.

He was in school uniform, so I could tell it was a student. His height was somewhat equivalent to mine, which suggested he's either in my grade or a grade higher or lower. I couldn't see his face quite that clearly. His hair...I felt like I had seen before.

The chase continued and I saw him rush downstairs. I screamed louder this time, "Stop it! Stop it I say!" but no response came from him.

It was the day of my swimming practice test and he had stolen my swimming bag! I could not let him escape, this was my only shot at swimming after all. So, I chased him further down another flight of stairs when he finally stopped.

Without turning around to face me, he rushed to the boy's washroom which was very close by, *with my* swimming bag. I hurried to the boy's washroom too.

The question was about my dignity and respect, and well, swimming. I obviously chose the latter, and burst into the boy's washroom.

I couldn't spot him! But everyone could explicitly see me. There were about four boys in that washroom, but personally, they seemed like a million. Four boys equaled eight eyes. I was standing in that washroom which seemed very unfamiliar, with eight eyes staring at me, and one pair belonged to the guy, who stole my swimming bag.

However, none of them had anything in their hand. Does that mean, I entered an unknown territory for no good reason? But if he wasn't there, where was he? That's when it hit me, what if he hid it in one of the cubical?

According to my watch, I had precisely twelve minutes before the test, and thus began my hunt for the swimming bag. I searched the entire washroom and failed to find it. That's when I saw the bhaiya who was responsible for the cleanliness of the washroom, open his supply cupboard. There, in the corner of the shelf lay my swimming bag.

I had made it in time! According to my watch, I still had about 120 seconds before the test began. I quickly paced towards the swimming pool which was another floor lower.

Now only if I could find who stole my bag and why?

❀ ❀ ❀

When I reached the swimming arena, I told Ms. Yadav that I'll go and change in a minute. I went inside the changing room and started to take out my swimming gear one at a time. That's when I found a note. *Again.* It read:

"Dear Sana,

I was told you are trying a hand at swimming. I am hoping that you found your bag after the test...it'll save you the embarrassment of not qualifying.

Love, Natz."

HOW DOES SHE GET TO KNOW ABOUT EVERYTHING???? I wondered and kind of screamed within. There has to be someone who is informing her about everything I do because, this can't be a one man's act. There have to be more people who are helping her sabotage me.

"Are you coming out of the washroom anytime soon??" shouted Ms. Yadav from outside.

"Yes Ma'am."

I shoved the note back into my bag and rushed outside.

❀ ❀ ❀

Standing there, I found Mr. Jain and Ms. Yadav, along with a couple of teachers who I didn't identify (but they seemed like sports teachers). Mr. Jain held a stopwatch in his hand, while Ms. Yadav had a notepad. That's when I realized, *they were going to time me!*

That's what was missing the entire time. Throughout the weekend I did practice, but I never practiced by timing myself. So, I had no clue how to answer, when Ms. Yadav popped the question, "What is your average timing Sana... for freestyle?"

My average timing. Right. Uh...what's a good timing? I thought. What was there to think? I had no clue. So, I decided, it's better to come clean. I simply told her I have no clue what my average timing is and that I don't really know what's a good timing either.

All teachers gave me a look that I had been getting ever since I joined this school. The look of disapproval and disappointment. Before I knew it, the teachers sitting in the background started to talk in hushed voices.

Mr. Jain said, "It is okay Sana."

"Today, we are testing you only to see where you need to improvise and how much of work you need to do before the districts, that is if we feel that you are qualified to go for districts of course" Ms. Yadav told me.

Next, she explained to me what I am expected to do. What she told me was pretty basic, "You have to do all the strokes you know, which I am assuming are breast, back and free style, one after the other, 50-meter sprints" I smiled, that was easy! That's what I did on the weekend too. She continued, "But let me remind you, you only get maximum of 15 seconds max, to turn around and continue. Got it?" She continued in a hushed tone "Although 15 seconds is a lot too, but well."

15 seconds!? What was I? Some super human? When I practiced, I recall taking breaks of about a minute after every lap. How was I expected to cut down *45 seconds*?

26

THE PRACTICE TEST!

At that moment, I had only a little hope lingering in the back of my mind. I could feel the calm and tranquil water stare at me with pride. It seemed so certain, of not letting me get through this. It seemed so massive. Huge enough to engulf me into it, while I cry for help.

I closed my eyes, trying to block the view, but it persevered in my thoughts. I tried to erase the image, in order to calm my mind. Though, I couldn't do the same with the sound. The excess water, gushing through the canals, how could have had possibly blocked the sound?

That's when I heard the whistle blow loudly. I opened my eyes, and there again it remained, the massive pool ahead of me. And the only competitor it had, was me. As I stepped onto the block, I had completely blacked out, but before I knew it, I was in the water, making my way to the end.

Not long after, I found my head between my arms that were endlessly rotating one after the other, in a motion which made it seem like my right arm was chasing the left. My legs were doing something similar, but they were not rotating, they were kicking the water, and helping me move forward.

When I reached the end, I gasped for air, trying to inhale as much as possible in those brief few seconds. Before I knew it, I was doing the next stroke. My hands were now performing a completely different act. They came together, and jerked forward, tearing apart the layers of the water. My legs were replicating a frog or a toad, which made me feel like one too. I was so small in comparison with the gigantic pool. I felt like a lost frog in the middle of the giant ocean.

When I reached back from where it all started, I realized my body was tired already. I tried to keep moving, without pausing for too long. My brain automatically changed to backstroke, the reliever. I finally had the chance to breathe normally. By this time although, my body had almost given up. I revitalized myself by using all the air my body had taken in during the backstroke, and put in all my energy in the final lap.

When I turned around to take my last lap, I could feel my hands become numb, and my legs were barely functioning. My head was spinning by then due to all the water I had taken in. By now, I could see the end wall, covered in blue stones, looking straight at me. Those blue, shiny tiles, were the only thing that kept me going. I knew I was about to reach, and I did.

When I got out of the water, I wanted to shout and say, "I did it!" but instead I was huffing and puffing, trying to strengthen my body, to avoid another *fainting situation.*

I could hear my heart in my ears, thump loudly. I could tell I was breathing very noisily. I looked at Ms. Yadav and Mr. Jain, who were both engrossed looking at the notepad in Ms. Yadav's hand.

They were talking softly, so I squinted my eyes, trying to lip read, but I couldn't really make out what they were saying, however, they did not seem as satisfied as I was. Ms. Yadav was shaking her head at something Mr. Jain had said, and Mr. Jain was scratching his head and ruffling his *hair* (which didn't really exist) in a funny manner.

I smiled at the other teachers and quickly went to the changing room to grab a towel, otherwise I would've have frozen. When I came back, they were both waiting there, staring at me. I stepped closer to them, hoping they'd say something.

Ms. Yadav bit her lip, in a way that said, 'I'm tensed and irritated.' She gave one final look to Mr. Jain. He too seemed nervous. It felt like although he was the boss, Ms. Yadav got to make this decision.

He looked at her intensely, it felt like they were communicating without words. I could tell they were still uncertain.

"You qualify... Barely," murmured Ms. Yadav.

I closed my eyes, capturing the moment. I stood there, letting the happiness soak into my bones. I could feel the power of joy cure all my worries, and pains. For a minute, I forgot that I had an enemy who was trying to hurt me. I forgot that I have lost all my friends. I even forgot that my life was a misery. All I could think of was the fact that I qualified. *I made it through something.*

The Burning Truth

Even if this test was unnecessary, and of no importance, I at least felt the joy of winning and making it through. And that point, it meant the world to me.

However, my brief moment of happiness was interrupted by Ms. Yadav's stern voice asking, "Wouldn't you like to know why I said *barely*?"

I felt like telling her, that I *barely* cared about her 'barely.' All I wanted to remember from this moment was that I made it. That I too was capable of something. But then, reality struck and I had to reply, "Uhhh...yes ma'am. I was about to ask, what do you mean by me barely qualifying?"

Without any hesitation, they both started to tell me all the areas that I needed to work upon. Their first point was obvious and understandable, *I had no stamina.* Then it seemed like they were just using terminology which made no sense to me for some reason. Ms. Yadav said, I needed to work upon my 'Stroke glide' and my 'starts and flips' and then Mr. Jain suggested, you need to really buckle up when it comes to 'The six-beat kick.' *The what now?*

Ms. Yadav further told me about the most dreaded part, "Your timing...it's okay. I mean, you really need to work hard on it. Every swimmer needs to. Your timings were umm...41 seconds Freestyle, 43 seconds back and 46 seconds breast. So, based on this, we both suggest for you to take up Freestyle as your primary stroke."

I didn't have much to say. Because, I didn't really know if the timings were good timings or bad. Nevertheless, I nodded at them and said, "Anything else ma'am?"

She looked at me and raised an eyebrow. "You obviously need to polish your strokes."

Mr. Jain extended his hand and said, "Welcome to the Team, Sana."

Ms. Yadav firmly spoke, "Tomorrow morning, report for practice at 6."

I could hardly express my happiness. I felt as if it was all just a dream, *a good dream*, after a long time. It felt like the storm was finally over and the rainbow was now clearer and visible.

If only had I known at this point that this was just the deep breath before the plunge.

27

RIA'S WRETCHED REALITY

Mumma jumped with happiness, I hadn't seen her so happy in a very long time. She hugged me tight and I could feel her spicy floral perfume run down my nose. "This is amazing Sana!" she said excitedly.

"I know... I mean, when she said that...you qualified, I couldn't believe it. It was...it was like a dream."

"Well, now you know, dreams come true. All you've got to do is work towards them." She replied, with a smile.

I smiled back at her and went to my room. I was exhausted by then. My limbs had given up, and my head was heavy too. My face was pale and my eyes had a lining of red on them. My hands were wrinkled because of the long hours in water, and the only thing I wanted to do was hop onto my bed, pull up my cozy blanket and sleep. But instead, I got into my blanket and pulled out my phone.

Once I opened WhatsApp, I realized, Ria had still not replied to my text. Maybe she really did block me. I had had enough, so I decided to call her. When I did, her number was going busy. I kept trying repeatedly and It kept going busy. I didn't get it. Why was she doing this? *Did she block my number completely?*

That's when I thought of something that I now regret incredibly. I opened Instagram and logged in from my fake account that I used to stalk people if they've blocked me. I opened her account (which was thankfully not private) and the first thing that popped on my screen, was what ruined my entire day.

Her latest post was a picture of her along with my Renuka and all my other past minions and some of my old friends at Starbucks, Cyber Hub. It wasn't exactly a picture of their faces, it was just their drinks with their names on them (*typical Starbucks snap*). Looking at the image was surely hurtful, considering that they never even tried to contact me, but what hurt me even more was the caption which read:

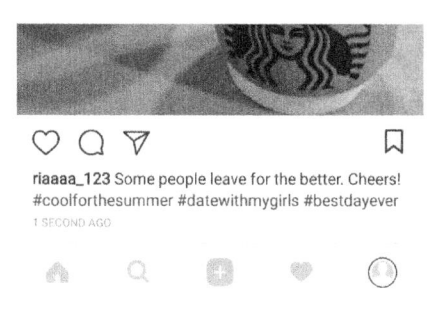

riaaaa_123 Some people leave for the better. Cheers! #coolforthesummer #datewithmygirls #bestdayever
1 SECOND AGO

What was I supposed to think of this? There was no excuse that I could make up for consoling myself this time. I knew she was talking about me. Is it possible, that all this time, *she was simply waiting for me to leave...to take over my empire? Did our friendship mean nothing to her?*

A tear ran down my red eyes, and fell onto my phone screen. I shut it down, and wiped it on my pajamas. That's when my eyes came across the picture of Ria and I that was stuck on my pin board, with fairy lights surrounding it. It was a bright polaroid from the time we went to our first movie outing together.

We were both wearing identical tops and ripped jeans. I was making horns behind her head, and she was giving me the typical, 'Stop it or I'll kill you' look. I loved that picture. It perfectly described our relationship, *but we didn't have a relationship!*

I stood up from my bed and paced towards the pin board, ripped off the picture and tore it into pieces. Forming a cup out of my hands, I put all the tiny pieces of the picture into it. I took them to the washroom, and flushed them all down the pot. I saw the last remains of us, swirl down the pipe with the force of the water. Each piece disappeared one after the other, each memory fading away, one after the other.

That was the day I realized, there's no such thing as best friends forever, because *nothing lasts forever.* Things always fall apart eventually. Even if we don't want them to, and there's not much one can do about it. There's no one we can blame for it, and that's just probably how life works.

The next morning was a fresh one, it was my first day for my official swimming lessons. I woke up at 5 am that day since the team practice started at 6 am. That meant, we were going to *only swim* for a straight two hours.

Mumma forced me to fill my stomach, so once I was dressed and had gulped down a bowl of milk and cornflakes, Mumma and I headed for the car, that was because I had recently learnt that those who come for morning practices used private transportation.

Thus, began the longest car ride in the history of mankind.

28

LONGEST CAR RIDE EVER

She gave me around a minute and a half before she started the rapid-fire round. That was precisely the time it took for us from our home to the exit of the society.

The minute our car crossed the black and yellow speed breaker that was placed right before the exit gates; while the guards dressed in navy blue uniform saluted us, she started to give justification for why we needed to talk.

"You know you've been very distant lately. Although I'm glad that you told me all about the Natasha problem."

"So...that means I *haven't* been distant, *right*? Because... I told you about the Natasha thing."

With a perplexed face she replied, "Umm...no. What I meant was that it's great you told me about her, but you never told me about all the other things which have been going on in your life."

I knew she wouldn't stop unless I tell her something or the other. So, I told her to step on the gas, and ask whatever she wanted to know.

The Burning Truth

"Alright, what's happening between you and Ria these days?"

I decided to tell her a refined version of my sob story. "Before I say anything, let me tell you that this is no big deal, and I'm fine."

She seemed a little puzzled, "Alright...lay it on me."

"Okay, so the day I left school, I first texted this guy Aman, about it. By the time I got the chance to text Ria, I couldn't. I don't know the reason, but whatever. We haven't talked ever since and I'm cool with it being that way."

She seemed unconvinced but she continued, "Fine... what about your friends here?"

What was I supposed to tell her about this? I had nothing to say. If I have no friends, what would I say about them? I wanted to tell her that I had no one to talk to at school. No one to sit with during lunch. In most cases, I was left isolated in a sad corner of every class which was not only affecting my academics, but even my mental health. *And all because of... Natasha.*

My only 'friend' or rather people I talked to were: the kid from the bus – Ansh and my buddy – Dev and maybe the other new girl from Shimla. The saddest part was the fact that, just because I stood up for myself, and told Natasha she was wrong, as well as revealed her insecurities, she was giving me the slow death treatment.

Every time something good happened like getting a good form tutor, or doing well in a subject, I knew that it would be followed by something horrible. And even though I was still not accepting it, deep down I knew, that *I was becoming scared of happiness, for I knew what was to follow.*

But I didn't mention any of that. I put it down in a more concise and *less* saddening manner. In a soft voice, I told her, "I am in the process of making friends. One does not make friends *overnight*, right?"

"But it's been almost a month since you joined." She argued.

"Yeah...but it takes time. And I'm getting to it, eventually."

There was silence. So, I used the time to stare outside the window, and I recalled the day when we were going for my interview. I remember thinking, *this school is a f*cking five-star hotel!* But now that I go to that place every day, I had started to see its flaws.

I thought about the food which often had flies either hovering or sitting right over them, and then, leaving us with no option but to consume the same food because of the crunch of time. I thought about fake promises they made about things that attracted me like golf and horse riding. Plus, how could I possibly forget those identical staircases and corridors without any sign boards that could easily swamp a new child in themselves?

I started to think about the minute problems that I faced from day to day, but before I could dive into deeper thought, Mumma popped the next question.

"How are your...teachers?

My teachers? What was I supposed to tell her about them? I mean they were all so mean and scary on my first day, and just about every one of them scared me down to the spine.

Hence, I tried to think about all the good things that had happened to me. I thought about the time we were working in pairs during Chemistry, and I ended up with no partner. So, Ms. Naarain, my chemistry teacher decided to team up with me, and boy, *it was fun.* Then, I thought about my physics teacher who was also a good teacher. While he failed to handle the class in most cases, no matter day or night, he was always there to support me and answer all my endless questions before the unit test prior that week. And then there was Ms. Sehgal, of course.

Finally, I assimilated all my views and told Mumma, *"There are always going to be different types of teachers. Some are good and supportive, while some are less good and supportive. But at the end of the day, they are teachers, and their duty is to simply impart knowledge."*

By then I think Mumma had had it. She slowed the car, looked at me in the eye, smirked a little and said, "Stop giving me these political...diplomatic answers of yours. I know everything. I'm your mother, don't you see?"

I chuckled a little and said, "I see."

As I said that, I saw the school building glimpse from between the trees that covered it. I picked up my bag that lay on the floor of the car and we did our goodbyes. As I was about to shut the door close, Mumma stopped me.

"Wait. Umm... There was something important that I had to tell you."

"So? Tell me?"

"Well, I don't recall."

"Tell me lat-"

"No, it was important."

I was getting irritated because my watch read 5:56 and that meant I had precisely four minutes to run across the gigantic football field, down the flights of stairs and into the swimming arena. I impatiently gave her a look and then she finally spoke, "Your father is returning tomorrow from his trip."

Shit! He had no clue about the whole swimming thing, and Natasha thing and basically anything that was going on in my life.

I let out a sigh, "A month is over already?"

"Yup."

"Well, we'll figure out a way to tell him, when he's in a good mood perhaps."

"Okay beta." She said with a partially convinced expression.

I hurriedly shut the door behind me and waved at her one final time.

29

GOOSEBUMPS

"Don't stop! Keep running!" said Mr. Jain standing in the center of the football field which now seemed even bigger, since I was running on it. I was putting in maximum effort, but even then, it felt like I was on a treadmill which kept me stagnant in one place, regardless of how much I tried.

I remember in flashes, that it had rained the night before, and so the mud too was doing a good job at decreasing my speed. With every step I took, it slowed me down even more. Then came the misty, wet grass. Which although gave the *petrichor*, the earthy smell, which I loved, it too had ganged up with the mud against me. I tried to run, but the grass made me slower and tired.

I saw most kids overtake me one at a time, and I knew I couldn't take it any longer. So, I tried to combat the mud, the grass and everything else that was stopping me from going faster. I took steps as long as possible and tried to imitate runners who I had seen on TV. And surprisingly, even though I wasn't the first to finish the laps, I was not the last either.

We were a total of twelve students who were being trained to head for the districts. Out of these twelve, I recognized only seven of them, since they were from my grade. The others seemed a little younger than me, but they were good too, and some of them were much faster than us 9th Graders. The ones who I recognized included my buddy, Dev; the girl from my bus, the girl whose profile I stalked - Gamini Khanna and two more guys who I had seen on Ansh's Facebook profile.

All of us then headed for our dryland exercises which included stretches and things that were supposed to help us with swimming. Even though I realized that the practice was getting harder, so was my body because, by the end of the stretches and the sprints, although I was incredibly tired, I was, for a change, not fainting like I did before.

Once I was done with my main sets wherein I was trying to master my freestyle stroke, I looked at the clock hanging on the white walls that caged the swimming arena, which read, 7:59. I could hardly notice that the needles had switched places, and two hours had passed by so soon.

I quickly changed into my school uniform and rushed upstairs to avoid being late for attendance. I remember that day, everything had been running so smoothly, that I got goosebumps because I knew something bad was about to happen.

❀ ❀ ❀

I was alone, as usual, and was running down the staircase, headed for my design lesson when the guy from the bus, Ansh, 'accidentally' bumped into me. I was about to showcase my reflexes which included me shouting at whoever bumped into me, and telling them to never show me their face again, but then I saw him and I realized, that I wasn't at FPS anymore. I've got to be nicer.

So, being the nice person, I smiled at him and said, "I am so sorry Ansh."

"Oh please! *I* bumped into you, *I* should be saying sorry."

Thank God, he realized that, if he wouldn't have accepted it, I would have probably died thinking, what's wrong with the guys of our generation? Why don't they ever accept when they are wrong?

"It's fine...totally fine." (It wasn't... But I was probably going to be late for my next class because of him, so I chose to say it's fine).

He suddenly had a weird grin on his face, "Wait a minute, there are no sorrys among friends." He hesitated and continued, "I mean, we are friends...right?"

Were we friends? Did I want to be his friend? I considered my options and realized, I didn't really have many at Avenues. Plus, he seemed decent enough so I smiled and said, "Of course!"

As soon as I said that, his face was filled with triumph and pride, as though he had accomplished something big by making friends with a commoner and infamous girl like me.

We started to walk together towards the design labs which were one of my favorites at Avenues. These labs were always full of life, in some odd corner or part of the lab, one could always hear a machine chopping wood, slicing sheets, printing designs and shaping models. Every time I entered the design lab, I felt like I had been gifted this super power that allowed me to create anything and everything.

Ansh and I weren't exactly in the same design lesson, but we were on the same floor. Co-incidentally, I realized when we reached my class, that my teacher was yet to arrive. So, I thought *what's the harm in talking a little more*? I went inside, dropped my bag and came back.

He waited by the entrance of the class, leaning against the door. His hair was ruffled, his eyes were dimmed, he stood tall and with his shoulder wide, clicking his fingers, seeming a little restless.

"Want to walk around for a while?" I asked curiously.

"Sure...sure."

We started to take rounds of the area. And there was a brief moment of silence when he hesitantly said, "So...my birthday is coming up soon."

What did he expect me to do about that? Why would he even tell me that? He probably just said it to make this 'new friends' thing less awkward.

"Your birthday is coming soon...and?"

"And...I was thinking of throwing a party and stuff. No big deal though."

"So...?"

My mind started to cook up stories and make connections immediately. My mind legal pad was out once again and I was thinking of whether I should say yes

The Burning Truth

or no if he invited me for this thing. I started to think of all the pros and cons. The list in my head looked somewhat like this:

Say YES! ☺	Say No ☹
He's a popular kid, he has many friends.	His friend circle (according to FB) is only popular kids = mean, arrogant and stupid
He's my only 'friend' and turning him down is basically a dumb move.	*But he is none of those –* Wait, that's a Say YES!
He's kinda cute. And nice.	Natasha *might* be invited too.
I can become a part of his friend circle too.	Convincing Papa to let me go would be super tough.
If I reject this, I might never be invited for anything ever again	
It's my only chance to make friends.	

I was deep into my legal pad zone when he finally replied, "So...you wanna come? It'll be fun..."

I needed time to think! How can he be so direct? UGHHH!

"You're asking me if I want to come for the party?" I tried to stall him.

"Yes Sana, I'm inviting you to my *yet to be planned* birthday party."

I didn't know what to say! Does he want me to give an answer right away? I mean I needed to talk to Mumma and Papa first. But what if he thinks that's *uncool?* You know...still asking for permission when I'm in ninth grade. *What if that's not how it works at Avenues?* And if I said, I needed time, he'd probably think I'm saying no. and that could affect our friendship. *Should I just change the topic or something? That's just dumb, it won't work.*

I have to decide. Right now. *Well, if I looked at the pros and cons, it says that I should obviously say YES but then...if Natasha's going to be there, it'll be a disaster. Plus, convincing Papa is way too difficult.* So, I made my decision. *A decision that was about to change my life.* Forever.

"I'll be there...for your yet to be planned birthday." I smirked.

His face became bright, and he was once again smiling like he always does, showcasing all his teeth.

"That's great Sana!" He was still smirking, and had started to step backwards, facing me.

We were getting further away from each other. He continued to take small steps backwards effortlessly, without looking where he was headed. He finally said, "So, I'll catch you later?"

I blinked my eyes and smiled at him, and then waved him goodbye.

Now, all I needed to do was figure out: *how do I convince my parents to let me go...*

30

PAPA'S UNUSUAL SIDE

I woke up because of the doorbell that was ringing loudly in the background but I lay in bed, waiting for either the help or for Mumma to answer it. But it just kept ringing and no one went to open the door. The loud, piercing sound then started to give me a headache, so I tried to cover my ears using a pillow. But the sound travelled through the hall and the door, into my room, and past my pillow barrier and into my ears.

I couldn't take it anymore.

So, I stood up, keeping my eyes closed (otherwise my sleep would have been disturbed). Picked up my phone and headed out to the main entrance. The only light that was lit in the drawing room was a small lamp that was kept in the far corner of the room. I felt my way through and reached the door.

I barely opened my eyes to unlock the door which was loaded with various sorts of locks, *each* serving the *same purpose.* When I finally managed to open all six locks, I opened my eyes a little to see who on Earth was trying to destroy my deep sleep.

It was dark inside, and even dark outside the house. So, I couldn't really make out who was standing at the door. I took out my phone from the pocket and switched on the flashlight. It glowed on the man's face, and then I fathomed, it was *Papa* standing there.

My body woke up due to the shock it had received and a chill ran down my spine. He stood there dressed in a suit, with a suitcase in his hand, and although 98% of the time he looked angry, this time, he looked in an even worse mood.

"How come you're home so early? It's 3 at night Papa... and wasn't your flight supposed to land somewhere around 8 am?"

He looked at me with a strange face and murmured under his breath, "Shouldn't have let her give her opinion from the beginning." He continued, "What are you? A reporter or something? Asking me so many questions..."

I had seen him angry on several occasions, but for some reason, I could tell he wasn't angry. He instead seemed irritated and pissed for some reason. It seemed like he hadn't had the chance to sleep in days, and so he was now acting like a cranky baby.

Contemplating, I apologized to him, even though I knew I hadn't asked anything worth apologizing for, and I returned to my room to sleep.

The next morning, I woke up again according to my early morning swimming practice schedule. All was going fine, I had picked up my bag, had my Aamras in hand, and was about to leave for the car with Mumma,

The Burning Truth

until Papa stepped out of his room, still wearing his suit and tie.

I figured that he probably didn't have the energy to change into night wear. Nevertheless, his face clearly said, 'Where are you going? What are you up to?'

So, before he'd get the chance to ask either Mumma or me, I decided to tell him the reason myself.

"I have extra mathematics lessons, since I joined in new and you know...maths here is different. And then I have an additional lesson for Eco. That's because our teacher has been absent and we need to cover up our syllabus for the unit test."

He stepped closer towards me, and looked me in the eye, "Sana Sharma..."

Silence.

"Why are you giving me justification for what you're doing, when I didn't even ask you?"

How does he catch my lies every single time?

"Well, I just presumed that you're about to ask me where I'm going with Mumma, so I just told you first itself."

He raised an eyebrow and said inquisitively, "Oh really?"

"Yes Papa, and now, I'm getting late. Can I leave please?"

"Alright. Go. *Please* go. I'll see you in the evening." He said in the most sarcastic tone possible.

As soon as we got out of the house Mumma asked me why had I lied. I replied to her that I needed time to explain things to him, and I didn't have that much time in the morning. Plus, I told her about how he seemed excruciatingly grumpy from the night before and so I didn't want to endanger my life by breaking another bad news to him. Although she was first unconvinced, she eventually settled down by the time we reached school.

And once again, the daily grind began.

31

WRONG DECISIONS

A tiny off-white eraser brushed against my shoulder and landed on the table behind me.

"What are you daydreaming about, Sana Sharma?" shouted my Spanish teacher.

Ugh. It was the third time in the day since I had ended up being scolded by a teacher, because I was thinking about something else. This time, I won't blame the teacher, for shouting without any reason, because this time there was a reason.

The entire day, the only thing I had been thinking about was how would I tell Papa about everything that had been going on in my life. I knew that he'd hardly give a damn about my dying friend circle and my ruined social life, but I also knew that he'd not be happy with this whole swimming thing.

Since I was born, I was always told indirectly more often directly by Papa, *'the only key to success is good grades in academics.'* So, I had been working on that principle all my life, until this year - when I thought, 'okay, I sure do want success, but what about my happiness?' Thus, I decided to dig deeper into swimming, a thing that I thought would give me happiness.

Practicing for districts like mad rats was definitely tiring and painful, but it also gave me immense satisfaction and happiness. Maybe for a while, that's all what I needed. But I couldn't say that to Papa as he seemed to be clueless about what happiness is.

I myself can't seem to remember the last time I saw him smile. My Mumma says it was when I had won a spelling bee thing in third grade (what about all the other things I won after that??).

I kept thinking of ways to tell him throughout the day at school and I kept getting scolded from every teacher for being non-attentive.

At home, Mumma and I waited for a long time, sitting at the dining table, but Papa didn't return home. After finishing dinner, Mumma continued to sit with me and read a book, whilst I prepared for my coming unit test that was scheduled for the next day.

By the time the clock struck 12, my eyes had started to get watery, and my head was getting heavy. I realized I couldn't stay awake anymore, and so Mumma and I decided to finally go to sleep.

Srry couldn't tell u in person. When I came home, u were gone 4 work. Urgent work came up, im leaving 4 Dubai. Will brb by nxt week.

As I collected all my books and notebooks that

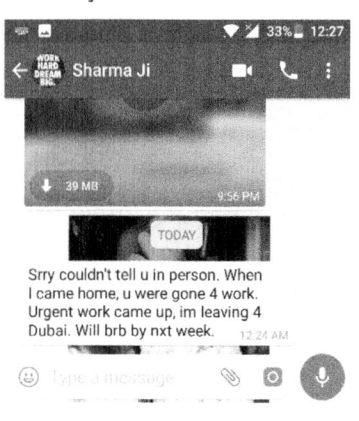

were spread across the dining table, Mumma suddenly grabbed my hand and told me she has a message from him.

I looked at her attentively, waiting for her to open the message. She took a deep breath and read the text out aloud.

I immediately started laughing at his way of texting, but I couldn't be happier! This meant, that I didn't need to tell him anything about swimming and the districts... at least until next week. And that's when I noticed, Mumma wasn't as happy as I was about Papa having to leave.

I asked her what was the reason behind her unhappiness and she replied, "Sana beta, you might be happy right now, but not dealing with the situation now itself would only aggravate and make the situation worse for the future."

I bit my lip out of tension and asked, "What are you saying?"

"What I'm saying is, that it'll be in the interest of all if you go and talk it out with him over the phone tomorrow itself or even now...but it's very late."

Maybe I was a little cranky and irritated because of being low on sleep, or maybe I was just tired because of the swimming practice, and the scolding, and the studying, that I made the *worst decision of my life*, I chose not to tell him that day itself.

As the saying goes, one wrong decision leads to another, and another, and another. Until you feel like your entire life is bad because of one wrong decision, which in my case was my parents deciding to put me at Avenues International.

I now wish that if my mom would've forced me a little...

Everything that was about to happen wouldn't have happened.

32

FLIP, TURN AND RUN!

"Alright people. Today we're practicing flip turns, which would help you in speeding up your game," said Ms. Yadav.

"First, Mr. Yadav show to you herself, then we see you all one by one. Understand?" added Mr. Jain.

We all scrambled across the swimming arena, to where our teachers were standing. We were then told to get into three lines. I tried to get a position towards the end, because unlike most swimmers, I had no clue of what a flip turn was. So, I thought to myself, if I am able to see a few students doing it, I'll be able to do it better. It was either that, or I was simply scared (even though the name 'flip turn' sounded kind of fun).

I stood there in line, listening to Ms. Yadav show us exactly what a flip turn is. We were watching her from above like sharp shinned hawks, who were waiting, and simply observing every move of hers. Soon, she dived into the water, covered a distance of somewhere around 25 meters, and then started to swim right back towards us. As she approached us with great momentum, she suddenly bent her head downwards, eventually curled up her body and then finished with the summersault.

An underwater somersault, where in you also kick the wall for more speed and momentum. *I can do that, I can definitely do that.*

Then I saw kids go into the pool one after the other, trying to master the flip turn as they received feedback from the coaches. The first swimmer that went in, gained too much momentum in the start itself, and ended up nearly banging his head into the wall, because he couldn't do the somersault. *That won't happen to me, right?*

The next swimmer was Dev, he did an almost perfect flip turn, but Ms. Yadav found a fault in that too. "Tuck your knees and legs tighter to your chest, make your ball tighter," she shouted at him.

The next child who went in, was one of the best swimmers of the team, he was called *the wave* and although it sounded funny, it pretty much suited him. He often did swim effortlessly like the waves. It seemed as though the water took him into its arm and gave him a ride across the pool. His flip was what I'd call, amazing. I was lost admiring his flip, when I heard my name being called out.

"Sana, you're up next. Get ready."

"Yes, yes." I hesitated.

I started to warm up by doing some stretches and all. I was nervous, because although I had been practicing since some days now, it was the first time when we were doing solos. I faced the water, and wished that I came out alive. Instead of practicing a 'flip turn' I might as well flip, turn and *run* away!

"Jump!" She screamed.

And before I knew it, I was in a streamlined position, diving into the water. As I approached the wall, what I saw in front of me, was not an ordinary swimming pool wall that was covered in blue stones, what I saw there was my path to victory, acclamation and applause.

So, I charged towards it, and I tried my best. My body curled up the way it often does on a cold winter night. Then my legs magically twisted and hit the wall, giving me a perfect push, and once again my body was in the streamlined position, jetting forward like an airplane, swiftly through the water.

❀ ❀ ❀

I was getting out of the swimming arena, when Ms. Yadav called me over to her.

"Ms. Yadav?"

"Yes Sana, I needed to talk to you."

Oh God, what now?

"Okay..."

"I saw your flip turn today, and... I have been seeing you practice your stroke glide and everything."

I nodded.

"Your flip today...it was pretty good! The only reason I didn't say it there was because, you know, it will boost your morale, but the others wouldn't have liked it."

"Oh, I understand. Thank you so much ma'am."

I can't believe it. Did Ms. Yadav just now praise ME? I was overwhelmed. It all felt like, impossible a little while ago. And now it's happening, I have improved!

She took both her hands, and placed them on my upper arm. "I am looking forward to good results from you, okay?"

From me? What about all those swimmers who are perfectionist, like The Wave, or the other new girl from Shimla, or what about the other student – Gamini? Why me?

"Definitely ma'am. I'll do my best."

We smiled at each other and that was an awkward moment. She finally broke the silence by saying, "Now off you go!"

33

THE IRRESISTIBLE INVITE

At home, I got dressed and sat down to practice Maths; when my phone buzzed. I ignored it for a while, since I was studying. I continued with my sums, but a few minutes later, it buzzed again. I had a Maths unit test the next day, so, I knew I couldn't afford to get distracted. Thus, I immediately put my phone on silent and continued to study.

A few hours passed by, and it was almost dinner time. That's when I looked at my phone at last. When I switched it on, the first thing that my eyes saw, were multiple texts from Ansh Roy. But why Ansh? That's when it clicked, he had said his birthday is coming up next week. Perhaps, it's about that.

My thumbs quickly navigated through the home screen, and clicked on WhatsApp. I saw a series of messages lying there, from my 'Family Group' which as expected, was mostly full of 'Good Morning' and 'Happy birthday' texts. I decided to skip through them and jump straight to Ansh's texts. They said:

As soon as I read all of the messages, I had multiple questions juggling in my mind. The most important one being, why the hell is there no time bracket? What is '7 pm *onwards*'? Plus, why did he choose to *personally* invite me? He could have simply broadcasted the message... And lastly, *The Rixton?* What is he? Like a Sheikh or something?

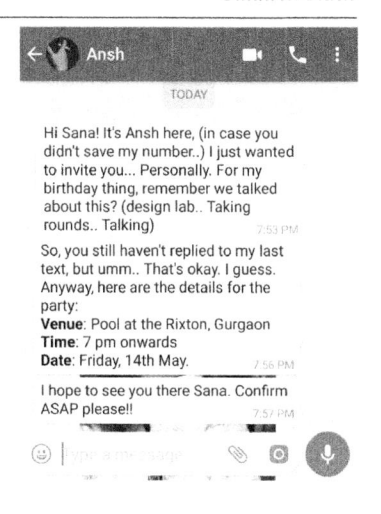

> **Ansh**
>
> TODAY
>
> Hi Sana! It's Ansh here, (in case you didn't save my number..) I just wanted to invite you... Personally. For my birthday thing, remember we talked about this? (design lab.. Taking rounds.. Talking) 7:53 PM
>
> So, you still haven't replied to my last text, but umm.. That's okay. I guess. Anyway, here are the details for the party:
> **Venue**: Pool at the Rixton, Gurgaon
> **Time**: 7 pm onwards
> **Date**: Friday, 14th May. 7:56 PM
>
> I hope to see you there Sana. Confirm ASAP please!! 7:57 PM

Also, if I were to go to the Rixton, then that would mean I needed a full makeover. New clothes and probably a bikini and a gift. Ugh, what will I gift him? Before all that, I first had to ask Mumma if I can go. I guess she'll be fine with it, as long as Papa doesn't return home that night.

I knocked on her door, and found her sitting on the bed working on her laptop.

"Mumma?"

"Yes Beta? Come in."

I went and sat next to her on the bed. I peeped into what she was working on her laptop and saw some spreadsheets and charts. *Parental stuff.* So, I waited awhile, for her to fixate her eyes on me, instead of her screen, but she didn't.

After a few minutes, I began to get restless, so, I finally asked, "Would you not like to know why I'm here?"

The Burning Truth

"Of course, I would, but I really need to work on this."

"Maa, please? This is important..."

She immediately put her laptop to sleep, looked at me, and curiously asked, "What happened Sana?"

I softly questioned, "Well, remember I told you about this guy Ansh, from the bus...?"

"Yeah, what about him?"

"He invited *me* to his birthday! And I really wanna go."

She looked bug eyed, and said, "Alright, sure beta. When is it?"

"Umm... This Friday, and that means I've got a lot of work to do before the birthday, I need to go to the sal–"

She interrupted me and her face suddenly became grave and dark, she sighed and with a sorrow face, said, "I was talking to your father, and he's coming back on Friday...early morning. And he made it very clear that he needs to talk to you about what happened that day, remember?"

"Okay, I'll talk to him. Don't worry. We'll sort this out, and then I'll go for the party."

She shook her head in disapproval and disappointment, as if she could predict something bad is going to happen.

"Alright Sana. But...I'm–"

I raised my voice and said, "No buts."

"Oh okay," she replied.

"So, I need to get a nice outfit, a new face, a good gift, and I basically need to look either better or like one of these girls..." I took out my phone and opened Facebook. I quickly scrolled down to find a picture from a recent get together Natasha and her friends had and showed their picture to Mumma.

The color drained out of her face. Her jaw dropped. "You're joking... I hope?"

"No Mumma, I'm serious. If I'm going to go for such a high-class party, then I need to dress up like them, act like them and behave like them. This is not FPS anymore and this is my only chance to get into their gang, make friends, get a life, so...please let me do this – I beg you mumma."

"Oh beta. I understand. And I am so happy...that this kid invited you. It's just...look at them." She pointed at the five girls who were sitting inside the cinema hall, next to each other. "They are barely wearing any clothes." She pointed at a girl who was sitting on the extreme corner. "Look at her...her shorts are so short that they hardly cover anything. And then look at this one... She is wearing a dress which literally says, *I'm faker than a Barbie.*"

I wanted to laugh, *my mom had sass!* She was quite accurate about that. But then... If I would have laughed, she would've thought otherwise. So, I showcased my stern face and said, "Mumma, please."

"Okay, okay. You can order whatever you want from Myistra. But nothing above 2k. Deal?"

"Two thousand? *That's it?*"

"Alright, 3 thousand. Not a single rupee more than that."

I hugged her tight, thanked her and went to my room.

Although I had said, I can handle Papa when he comes home, for some odd reason, I knew deep down that it's not going to end well. After all, I'd been keeping the whole swimming thing from him for over almost a month now. And if he really did get angry, *I knew bad things could happen.*

34

CHANGE IN PLANS

"AAAAAAHHHHHH"

"Oh my God! What happened?" I jerked up into a sitting position, on my bed.

There stood Mumma, screaming for some unknown reason. She glowered at me.

"What is wrong with you Sana?"

"What do you mean? I was simply sleeping here. Doing no harm to anybody. It is you who came and started screaming for no reason."

"Get up." She said bluntly.

"What? Why?"

"Just get up and look at your face in the god damn mirror."

That's when I saw my face, and I almost had goosebumps myself for a second. My face was covered in a dark green paste which made it look like I had green, slimy and disgusting algae growing all over my nose, forehead, cheeks and chin. That's when I recalled, that I had put a seaweed pack on my face before sleeping which promised to give me a *glowing, fresh and clean* skin the next morning.

"It's a face pack Mumma."

"For what?"

"For what?" I repeated sarcastically. "It's because today's Friday, the day of that party. And I need to look perfect."

"Right. Okay."

I was too embarrassed to continue the conversation any further, so I decided to rush to the washroom to wash off my face and to get ready for the morning, swimming practice.

At school, during our swimming practice, we followed our usual chores. By then, I had improved a lot. I noticed, that no more do I run out of breath when I start to run. In fact, I was being able to run either side by side, or right behind the best swimmers of the team.

During our warm up stretches, I didn't pull a muscle that often and I didn't end up breaking my bones every now and then too. And most importantly, I think I had really improved on the whole *fainting and stamina* thing.

But then, there's always scope for improvement. I was better than many in the team, but I knew that at the districts, I wouldn't be competing against children from my school or my team. Instead, I would be swimming with students from across Gurgaon and all schools like Shri Krishna, Basant Valley, Free-Lancers and many more. And I would be competing with them.

It was recovery time, when Mr. Jain came into the swimming arena with a sheet in his hand. He headed straight towards Ms. Yadav. Through gritted teeth he spoke, "I don't believe this. How can they change districts date in such tiny time? This not okay!"

Although his words rarely ever made sense, but by now, I had gotten used to decoding his special language. So, I could make out what he was saying was that the date for the districts have changed.

Ms. Yadav almost snatched the paper from his hand, and then looked at it. Her forehead puckered, and her eyes widened. "How can they do this? This makes no sense! They can't simply *prepone the districts by a whole month* itself!"

ONE MONTH. How can they make such a drastic change in dates? Although, what did that actually mean? How much time did we have to prepare, I thought. I mean, I have so much to work upon. Especially my dives, and they make such a great difference. UGHH.

Ms. Yadav stepped closer to us and read out the notice that had come from the 'Swim India Organization' which was hosting the districts. It said:

"Dear Participating school,

This is to inform you that the district level swimming competition that was to take place on the 15th of July, will now take place on the 15th of June, due to internal reasons.

Hope this has caused minimal or no inconvenience.

Regards,
Swati Chadha
(On behalf of Swim India)"

I quickly did the Maths and realized, that I barely had a month to get ready, and I had so much to do. I looked around myself, and saw that just about everyone was looking as scared as I was. Someone was biting their nails, while the others were clutching their heads.

Nevertheless, looking at everyone feel equally frightened, it calmed me down a little. At least that's what I thought.

Recovery time was over, so we all headed quickly to the changing rooms, to get ready. When we did finally come out, Ms. Yadav told us to wait.

Mr. Jain stepped out of his office, and they both called us all to huddle around them so they could talk. They had an announcement to make.

Mr. Jain started, "Ms. Yadav and I talked right now. We is made a decision."

Ms. Yadav butted in, "Since, the districts date has been moved up the calendar, we need to put in more effort. And the school can't give us more than three hours. So, we want to advise you all to take extra lessons outside the school. We'd be contacting your parents about the same soon. This may seem a lot, two hours morning practice, regular lessons during the day, and weekend lessons, along with these extra lessons outside school."

"But it's for your good only." Mr. Jain added.

"Exactly. And this time, we want at least five of you to qualify for states." As she said that, she even looked at me. Now, I might be simply over thinking, but it seemed like she was expecting *me* to qualify for the states. Whatever the case might be, I knew that I will have to persuade Mumma and Papa for extra lessons *before* they get a call or mail from Ms. Yadav.

35

GET, SET AND WAIT

When we were riding back home, in the bus, Ansh stopped by my seat. He took my school bag that lay next to me and sat down.

"How was your day?"

"Tiring."

"Oh, why?" He seemed concerned.

"Well, just like that. Anyway, all set for your umm... party?"

"Yeah...uh, all set, except one thing, you *never* replied to my text!"

Oh shit. I was probably so happy and then the whole conversation about Papa and clothes and everything. It made me forget to reply. What should I tell him?

"Umm... I didn't? That's so so so...strange."

"Yep, very strange. So, are you...coming?" He said with an eyebrow raised.

Words stammered out of my mouth, "Of course... I am."

"Really?" His flashes fluttered.

"Really." (*Was this our Okay? Okay. Moment???*)

He gave me the same 'full of teeth' smile I saw on my first day and replied, "Okay, see you at 7 then."

"Yeah. See you Ansh."

The minute I got home, I started to get dressed. I had ordered a plain black dress, with a sequenced neckline. It was above the knees, because I realized that no one. By no one, I mean, even the fat ugly girls at Avenues, don't wear anything below knee length.

I borrowed Mumma's black and silver stilettos to wear along with the dress, but from the second I wore them, they started to bite my feet and cut my heals. I felt as though I was standing two stories above ground level, and it was a rather bittersweet feeling.

From my long lost hidden treasure, I found a temporary hair color spray, using which, I gave my hair tips a touch of bronze or dull gold color. Then, a quick google search told me how to put up my hair in a messy bun, I left out a few strands of hair straying loose from the bun. Some of which I left hanging and the rest I tucked behind my ear.

I didn't really have much clue about makeup, so I ended up asking help from Mumma. She insisted that too much make up would make me look like an adult, but when I showed her pictures of Gamini Khanna and Natasha, and the amount of makeup they applied even when they came to school, she settled for an eye liner, some foundation, highlights and lipstick.

Then came the hardest part, finding the right accessories. It was difficult, because I couldn't understand what to wear exactly. Something that doesn't seem showy, but also shows class. Something that suits the dress but also goes in contrast. I finally wore tiny star shaped silver earrings which, to me, quite honestly, looked just right.

When all was done, I took out my silver sling that went quite perfectly with my dress and packed in my phone, a lip gloss, a hair band, and my wallet.

I looked at myself in the mirror one last time, and in it I saw a person who looked nothing like Sana Sharma.

I was dressed and ready to go. I picked up his gift, and headed to the door of my room. As the door slowly swung open, I found him standing there, with his arms crossed.

For I was the mouse, and he was the dreaded cat, waiting to pounce upon me.

36

SHARMAJI VS. SHARMAJI KI BETI

He glared at me with eyes filled with fury. His nostrils flared, and the corner of his eyes crinkled. He tapped his foot on the floor, as if in a beat.

He then started to walk towards me. Without saying a single word, he started to scrutinize starting from the toe and gradually moving upward.

"So, correct me if I am wrong. But by looking at you, I can tell that you are headed out. Past 7 pm. On a Friday night."

"Yes Papa."

He lifted an eyebrow and pressed his lips. He looked away from me and started to stare at the floor. It seemed like he was planning his next move, but he didn't say anything. It felt like he was giving me the silent punishment.

"Papa, can I please go. It's a friend's birthday and I don't want to be late."

He stopped staring at the floor, and turned around. He went and sat on a chair from the dining table, facing it towards me.

The Burning Truth

"You can go."

I started to walk towards the door.

Before I could make my exit, I was stopped by papa as he added a clause, "Only after you tell me where you were headed that day, early in the morning, at 6 am!"

"Papa, I promise, I'll tell you everything, but let me go right now. This party means a lot to me."

All of a sudden, he lost it. He stopped being mysterious and quiet. He stood up from his chair, came and grabbed me by the hand, and pushed me towards the sofa screaming sternly.

"Sit down."

I remained standing, and looked at him with a blank arrogant face. I was determined to leave.

"Alright then, don't sit but listen up Sana Sharma. No *party* can be more important that your *father.* And you have been trying to negate this conversation since a long time now. So, it's now or never."

"Oh, so *I have been trying to negate this conversation*? Is that how you're putting it Papa?"

"I think I made myself clear on that already."

"Papa I wanted to tell you that day itself, but it was you who vanished when I came back," I said calmly.

I raised my voice and continued, "Are you ever there to talk to me? Are you ever there at all? I was there. I was waiting. We were both waiting for you Papa...until 1am that night."

"I went for work! God dammit." he shouted back.

"Oh... God. The same excuse every time. I went for work. I went for work. We all know you went for work. But how did you tell us that you're gone for another week? Through a text. A text message Papa! Not even a call?"

Mumma came and stood between us. "Alright you both, I think we are going completely off topic here."

He gave the look he gives to Mumma every time he wants her to shut up, and like always, she did. *Why mumma?*

"Look, all I want to know is what's going on in your life. What 'secret' thing are you doing that needs to be hidden from me?"

"I am *not* hiding anything from you. And even if I was, there would be a reason."

He sighed and said, "Alright then, just tell me the truth. Where were you headed that morning? Because I called your school, and there were no extra classes Sana."

"So, you stealthily went behind my back and checked what I was saying was true or not? Seriously? You don't even trust me *that* much?"

"Oh please, after all, you were lying, weren't you?"

"Alright, I'll tell you where I was. But once I do, *you* are going to let me go for that party."

"Fine."

He finally sat down on the sofa, showing that he was ready to hear what I had to say.

"Okay, so, I'll keep it short and simple."

"Hmm."

"I have had a liking for swimming. I was a 'natural' swimmer according to my coach. They felt that if I work hard, I can apply for districts and probably qualify for state level swimming too. So, that day... I was going for my early morning swimming practice."

His brows knitted together and his eyes narrowed.

"*Swimming?* So, all this while, you have been going for extra swimming lessons in the morning?"

"Yes. And that's all. Can I leave?"

"Stop asking me that."

"You promised that I can leave after I tell you everything. And that *is* everything."

"No! That is not."

"Oh my God. Let me go!"

"You don't want me to get physical here. So, it's in the interest of us all if you just sit. Now."

I looked at Mumma and saw her frightened face. I knew that if I stepped out of the house, he'd probably get angry at her. And then they'd fight...*because of me*. So, I sat.

"Okay. What did I not tell you, *please enlighten me.*" I asked him.

"Oh great. So, now my fifteen-year-old daughter would talk sarcastically with me." He questioned me.

"No, I was serious."

His face turned red, and his eyes blazed. He shouted, "In what mind did you decide to take up swimming, putting your *academics* on the side? And did you not even consider it a little important to ask for *my* permission?"

I thought if he could be angry, so could I. Ultimately, I shouted back, "I have *not* put my academics on the side. And what proof do you even have to say that? In fact, I am doing equally well, or even better in some of my subjects now. And I did want to ask you, but I was scared of...*this* Papa."

He yelled, "Scared of what?"

"Of you. Of this. What else?"

He shook his head, "What do you even mean?"

"What I mean is, that I knew this is how it would end up. I knew you'd want me to quit. I knew that we'll have this uncivilized conversation where you barely listen to what I have to say, what I care about, what is my opinion."

"When did I tell you to quit Sana?"

"Oh, so are you saying I should continue, because I'd love to continue. But you are suggesting that if given the opportunity, you'd tell me to continue rather than quit?"

"Why would I say that if I was in the right mind, unlike you? Of course, I'd tell you to quit. I don't support these stupid things, dancing, singing, sports, *swimming*. They are all useless and would get you nowhere."

I looked at him and shook my head in disappointment. "That is *exactly* the reason why I chose not to tell you at first. You...you are just unbelievable."

"I don't care what you think of me, I think I have made my point clear, Monday morning, first thing, you go and quit. I am not allowing this."

"Oh sure, I'll go right away and quit."

I picked up my things which I had kept on the dining table. And started to walk towards the door.

From behind me he shouted, "Where do you think you're going?"

"Exactly where you're thinking." I mumbled sarcastically.

"No. You are NOT going ANYWHERE tonight. Come back Sana Sharma." He screamed.

"Nothing and no one can stop me from letting me live my life. Not even you. This party means a lot to me, and it's my only key to a social life, a life for that matter. And even if I have to walk over your dead body to get to that do–"

He yelled, "Shut the hell up Sana! You have no idea what you're saying."

"No, you shut up." I shouted back.

My mom got into the middle of our pathetic fight that night, thankfully stopping me from saying any more crap.

I unlocked the door and stepped out. I looked back at him one last time before I left.

"I am leaving; and besides, you've lost me already."

37

ASHAMED OF ME?

I stepped out of the Uber that had brought me to The Rixton, at Ambience Gurgaon. The party was supposed to start at 7, but by the time I reached it was already almost 8:30. I walked in, onto the floor that was made using marbles in hues of brown and white; inside the huge building, and found myself standing in a lobby with magnificent fountains.

The fountains were only the beginning. Opposite me was a dazzling flower vase, which was taller than me in height too. For the finale, right above me was an enormous chandelier surrounded by multiple smaller chandeliers. Each part of it glowed, because of the light that shone through them, lighting up the surrounding area.

I was busy admiring the lobby when a staff member came and patted me on the shoulder. He was dressed in all black and had a kind smile.

"Miss, can I help you in any way?"

"Umm... Yes, yes, please."

The Burning Truth

I found my sling hanging on my shoulder, and took out my phone from it. I opened WhatsApp and found myself with 26 texts from Mumma. I knew she was worried. But, I skipped them all and went to the invitation Ansh had shown me.

"I want to go here... Um...for a pool party."

"Oh, so you are a guest of Mr. Roy?"

Whoa, they were so formal. I thought.

"Yes, Yes. I am his guest."

"Well, then it's an honor getting a chance to serve you Miss."

"Ohkay... So, umm...can you just guide me please?"

"Sure Miss."

He opened his right arm and gestured towards a corridor, "This way, please follow me."

As we were walking towards the swimming pool, I decided to take out my phone and check Mumma's texts. By then, I also had a text from Papa. So, I first checked his. My eyes welled up as I read the text which said.

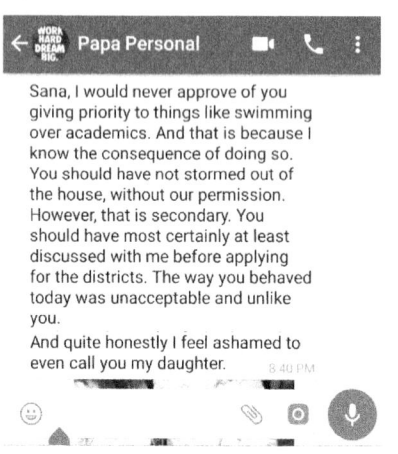

> **Papa Personal**
>
> Sana, I would never approve of you giving priority to things like swimming over academics. And that is because I know the consequence of doing so. You should have not stormed out of the house, without our permission. However, that is secondary. You should have most certainly at least discussed with me before applying for the districts. The way you behaved today was unacceptable and unlike you.
>
> And quite honestly I feel ashamed to even call you my daughter.

I fought back my tears, for I didn't wanted to be called the 'girl who cries at every party.' I shoved my phone back into my sling and dried my tears.

As I looked onto my right, I saw a sign board pointing at a glass door, that led to the swimming arena. The staff member who I was following opened the door for me, and passed me a big smile.

"This is it Miss. Enjoy."

I plastered a smile on my face and said thanks.

As I took a step outside the glass door, what I saw was a whole new world.

In front of me was a majestically sized swimming pool, with cabanas in the background, delicately decorated with fairy lights to set the mood. The pool was well lit too, with multiple bright lights shining on the trees that surrounded it.

The pool was filled with chic looking inflatable floats, some of which were in the shape of a sliced watermelon, a smirking emoji, a banana and peach emoji. On them lay a few girls who I had never seen before. And I could tell they were drunk because they were all trying to sink the floats (which are designed to *float*) with all their power. Plus, they were in the pool, with their clothes on, their hair and clothes drenched in water.

On the corner of the pool was a poolside bar, which was jutting out into the pool, with chairs that were fixed inside the water itself. What I didn't understand was how were they serving these high school and middle school students drinks when we are way below the age requirement.

The area was swamped with at least over 100 people ranging from grade 6–12th. While some of them were in the pool, and some were sitting by the bar, most of them were sitting in the cabanas, and to be honest, they weren't just sitting. Although from a distance, I couldn't see much, I could definitely tell that all those in the cabanas were behaving like adults & not teenagers.

Out of all these people, I knew only one person – Ansh Roy. Who I presumed was about to make an announcement as he was climbing the steps to the mini stage which had been strategically built in between the cabanas, overlooking the entrance to the pool, and the pool itself.

There were large speakers placed on that stage and in various parts of the grand arena, which were blaring 'Closer' by The Chainsmokers.

I decided to flee to the washroom to touch up my makeup which had been destroyed first at home, due to all the shouting and screaming and what not, and then the crying after the reading the text. I scanned the area, and saw a board for the washroom that was pointing at a staircase which went underground.

As I started to walk towards the washroom, I tried to look around and see if I could find anyone else who was either willing to talk to me and make friends, or simply nice enough to let me sit with them. And although I failed to find any desperate socialite like myself but I did find my mortal enemy – Natasha.

I stood there, staring at her flawless body, which she was displaying to everyone at the party very graciously by wearing a way-above-the knee length dress, with sections cut off at the waist, which made it seem like she was basically wearing a blouse and a skirt, making it even more sexy.

She lay there on the pool side bench, under the cabana, talking to all her friends who had flooded the area around her. I could tell that they were all laughing, and were happy. Some of them had glasses filled with what seemed like alcohol and mostly the others were smoking cigarettes. Then, I turned my head around and saw, almost every child there was either drinking, smoking, vaping or with a hookah.

I swear, if any adult was to come to that party at that point, they would think these tenth or to the most twelfth graders were not behaving like kids but more like young adults who were living the life we see in movies and on screen. The sad part was that it was only I who was still standing in a corner, with no one to talk to or no one to laugh with.

The washroom was not too far, so I headed straight down, before it was too late and my eyes start to flood. As soon as I reached the washroom, I rushed into a cubical, and shut the door close. I pulled the down the toilet seat cover and sat down. I hung my sling onto the hanger on the door, and took out my phone. My body wracked with an onslaught of sobs and tears, as I reopened the message from Papa that said *he's ashamed of me.*

Moans escaped my lips through the suppressed sound of hiccups as I thought about everything that had happened with me. I thought to myself again, why did I even choose to come here? How did I ever think that I'd make friends here? Why would anyone even want to be friends with a depressed, isolated, and full of shit person like me?

I felt the wetness of the hot salty tears fill up my eyes, I thought, *what is wrong with me and my life?*

38

INSIGNIA?

Someone was knocking rapidly on my washroom door.

I quickly wiped my eyes, but the tears continued to fall. My handkerchief was already wet with tears, so, with no option left, I took a piece of toilet paper and tried to dry up my eyes.

"I can hear you crying Sana" a bold voice said from outside.

I didn't reply, because I knew my voice was shaky and would tremble due the crying. I tried to control myself.

"Please open the door!" he said persistently.

It was the second time, when I realized that the voice from outside belonged to Ansh. *Why was he here? How did he realize that I was in here? How did he even get into the girl's washroom? Why would he leave his own party to follow me till here?*

"Ansh...is it you?" I asked trying not to cry.

"Yes Sana. Now would you please come out? I know that you're crying."

How did he know that? UGHH. He probably got to know because of my very obvious hiccups, or perhaps because of the flood that I had caused in the cubical from all the crying. Or maybe because my voice was shivering.

"I'm not crying Ansh. Go away." I tried to send him away.

"Fine. I'm leaving. Okay? Now would you just...come out please?"

I could hear him make fake thumping sound using his feet to show that he's gone. *Why was he doing this?*

I giggled a little and said, "You know I can still see your sneakers from the slit below the door."

It felt like I could hear him smile on the other side. "Oops!" He replied.

There was a minute of silence, neither him, nor I, said anything. The washroom was empty, so, I could hear him breathe heavily.

He finally whispered, "Can you come out now?"

I nodded, even though I knew he couldn't see me. I took one long breath and finally opened the door. And there he stood, dressed in jeans, with a t-shirt over which he wore a shirt. His hair perfectly done, to give him the 'I woke up like this' look.

I forced a smile, trying to prove that I didn't cry.

"What...what happened Sana?" He seemed concerned.

"Nothing."

"Oh please. You have wiped your eyes so much that they are red and swollen. You look pale, it doesn't take rocket science to tell that something's wrong."

"Nothing is wrong. Just...let me be." I was getting irritated.

"Look, this is my birthday. And so, I can't have anyone crying. So, if you tell me your problem, maybe I can help..."

I couldn't simply tell someone I am barely close with about everything that had been happening with me lately. But I also knew he wouldn't stop asking unless I tell him something.

"Okay. So, I came here...and I had a breakdown. That's all."

"Because of...?"

"Well, I came to your party. And I realized, that I hardly know anyone. Then, I looked around, trying to see if anyone looked open enough to you know...let me in."

"And?"

"And... No one did. I mean, the minute I entered, people started staring at me like I was a creep and I was unwanted. Plus...there are some family problems I had to deal with. That's all."

He grabbed my arm gently and looked me in the eye. "Do you trust me?" He muttered.

I wanted to say, *not really*. Because I had barely known him for a month. But then, he trusted me. He invited me to his party. He made friends with me when everyone neglected me because of that Natasha bitch.

"Yeah. I trust you." I forced myself.

The corner of his mouth turned up. "Then come with me."

He grabbed me by the arm and steered me out of the washroom, and navigated me through the crowd of people. We finally got to a cabana which was completely empty. Outside it, was a white board that said in bold words, 'Reserved for Mr. Roy.'

"Have a seat Sana. I'll be back in a second. I promise."

I nodded at him, and entered the dim lit, lavender scented cabana.

A few minutes passed and then he finally returned. He smiled, as he sat down on the chair opposite mine.

"I have something for you, something that would definitely uplift your mood."

Nothing could lighten my mood. My father has nearly abandoned me. I have no friends. No life. And the one thing I'm getting good at: swimming, *that too was about to be taken away from me.*

I faked a smile at him, "I don't really think that's possible Ansh."

"Oh, trust me this thing I have in my pocket, it does wonders."

What was he talking about?

"Umm...What?"

"This thing right here, it's magical. If you're sleepy and tired, it will wake you up. If you're nervous and freaking out, it will calm you down. It's like the salt and the pepper, the mantra, for a good conversation, for thinking more creatively, for working even harder, for when you're feeling lonely, for when you're with somebody. It's the perfect complement to reading, and to music. But most importantly, it's your seal to the outside world, the seal that says, 'Sana is matured and cool.'"

My face grew dark and serious, and I was bond to inquire, "And what is 'it'?"

He smirked, and slowly put his hand into his pocket, revealing a black box that was almost the size of a palm, on which it was written in golden letters: *Insignia.*

He pulled his bench a little closer to mine, almost erasing the space that was between us. He attempted to make me trust him more, his eyes glistened, and his hand reached mine. He looked me in the eye and asked, "*Have you ever tried smoking?*"

39

THE VIP ACCESS

"*Why would I smoke?*" I screeched in anger. "I'm sure there are better ways to uplift someone's mood. For instance, I'd rather have had taken a swim in this beautiful pool, but it's been invaded by all these people," I told him, staring at the pool.

"So, you're saying that you don't want to try one of the most premium and luxurious cigarettes...in the entire world?"

"Well, I didn't know that. But then, what's even the point Ansh?"

He squinted, and questioned, "What...Umm...What do you mean?"

I turned around, and asked back "I mean...all these people who are smoking, and drinking and doing God knows what...isn't it all illegal?"

"Well, it *might* be...but look at them. They are having fun, and here you are so depressed, you look as if you're on the verge of dying. Plus, this is my hotel, and *nothing is illegal in me empire.*"

"*Your empire?* And plus, you're exaggerating...I am just a little depressed."

"Oh really?"

"Really."

"Fine then, you wanted to make friends right, well then you've lost it." He said hastily.

I raised a brow, "Lost what?"

"*Lost your chance.* Your chance to make friends. To be a part of some group. Make more friends apart from me. You've lost it."

"I really don't know...what you're saying."

"Well, if you really want to make friends, *smoking is your VIP access.*"

For an extended second, my eyes remained steady and unblinking on his face. I tilted my head and looked at all those people who were having fun, enjoying, partying. Then I lay my eyes upon the pack of Insignia cigarettes, that was resting on the wooden table between our benches.

I tried to draw the connection and it did make some sense.

"VIP access?"

"Yeah. You know, when you go into any of these cabanas, smoking an insignia, they'll all think, *whoa.*" He sneered, "*That girl is cool, isn't she?*" He continued confidently, "And then they'll want to be friends with you!"

"No...No...No. It can't possibly be as simple as that."

The Burning Truth

"It really is. I mean think of all those movies, isn't someone or the other always smoking? And it's mostly the cool guy."

I nodded, but counter argued, "But on the corner of the screen in tiny little alphabets it always says, 'Smoking is injurious to health.'"

He raised both his hands in dismay, and let them collapse on his sides onto the bench, as though showing defeat. But, I knew he hadn't given up. He looked at me and said something that changed my life, "Think about that family stuff you told me about. *Don't you want to forget all that and just feel better about it for a minute?*"

I so desperately wanted to forget everything that had happened that day. I squeezed my eyes shut, and thought about how Papa was screaming, how I shouted back at him. Mumma butting in and getting shut down. Most importantly, Papa saying that he's *ashamed* of me even after I tried everything. My grades were just about perfect, the teachers who were humane enough to like someone, liked me. And I had been doing well. All that I did, without his will, was take up something that I actually loved and enjoyed, and he had a problem with that?

A solemn tear fell down my cheek; my body looked calm compared to how tangled and messy the state of my mind was and before I knew it, a waterfall was flowing out of my eyes, so, I tried to cover my face using my hands, barely making a difference.

He finally stood up, and made himself comfortable in the empty space next to me. He lent me his arm, signaling that I can lay my head on his shoulder, and as I did, he wrapped around his arm around my body. Then, he asked me once again, "*Just try one,* I promise it'll rub away all your sorrows, at least for tonight."

I waited there, with my head resting on his shoulder, and my body almost curled up alongside his, staring at the box of cigarettes which were sitting next to a crystal glass half-empty. It felt like my entire body was slowly shifting towards the box, trying to lift it up, and take a cigarette out, but my brain was opposing this action by standing right there, guarding the pack of cigarettes, telling me no. But sometimes, our heads aren't as strong we'd want them to be, thus *the heart often overpowers the head.*

40

THE TURNING (.)

I let a deep breath escape my mouth, as I clutched my hair and scratched my head a little, I finally give in and said, "I can't take this anymore." My eyes blinked furiously, and I added, "Just *give me one cigarette*, it won't do much harm."

"Now, that's more like it!"

A gigantic, never-fading kind of smile swept across his face. It felt like he had finally accomplished a great task, a task of a lifetime.

He quickly grabbed the pack of Insignia from the table and flipped it open. Inside that black matte bundle, were twenty cigarettes placed strategically and somewhat skillfully next to one another. He picked the cigarette in the first row, in the first position from the right, and handed it to me with a lighter.

My cheeks were flushed with red, out of embarrassment. I had no clue how to smoke a cigarette. My eyes drooped, and the corner of my lips turned down. He looked at me and read my expression. In no time, he took out another cigarette from the same box and took the lighter from my hand.

"I suppose you need some help?"

"A little bit." I mumbled.

"Alright, just look and listen to me carefully. It's three simple steps. *Take it, light it, smoke it.*"

"Okay. Light, take and smoke."

"The opposite. Umm...Never mind...let's just get to it... Now, First, you tamp the pack. I'm sure you know how to do that."

I didn't.

"Sure, sure, sure."

He gave me the sympathetic expression, "Oh Sana, okay look. This is a simple trick for making the cigarette smoother and lasting longer."

"Got it smooth and long." I repeated speedily.

"But, it only works best if the packet is unopened...So, I can tell you for next time–"

"There won't be one. It's just...today...I'm really done. So, just this once."

"Okay," He said sarcastically, as though he was sure that I'd crave for another one. "Just invert the box, and pat it against a table or your palm."

"Fine. Go ahead." I said quickly.

"Okay...now I'll take out a cigarette. Wait and watch."

He held the Insignia box in his hand, and flipped it open. He used his fingers to take out the cigarette a little, and as it emerged from the box, he used his teeth and lips, to take out the cigarette straight from the box.

"How did you do that?"

"It's an old trick, you'll learn it with time. But...looks cool, right?"

"Yeah..."

"Okay, now there are many ways to hold a cigarette. I'll tell you the simplest one."

He took the cigarette and kept it on his left palm. "You take it like this, in between your middle and index finger, and keep the filtered part towards you. Got it?"

"Okay."

"Okay...Now, put the cigarette in your mouth like this." He slid the cigarette into his mouth, with ease. It came all so naturally to him, as though he had been doing it since forever, he shifted it a little towards the right side of his lips.

"You can put it on any side.... your choice completely. But don't keep it in the center...that just looks weird." He continued.

"Okay."

He spoke with the cigarette in his mouth, making his words slippery and his vowels seemed mixed up, but I somehow made sense of them. "Final step, light it up! Just bring the lighter close to your cigarette, and it's lit!"

"Got it. Now my turn?"

"Whoa, you're in a rush."

"Yeah, I just...need to relax. I have too much on my shoulders right now."

"Okay, here you go. Your turn Sana."

I did as he told, and I had finally chosen which side suits me best, I positioned the cigarette towards the left side of my mouth and it stuck there like a man, hanging from a cliff. I took the lighter and tried to turn it on. But nothing happened, that's when I was told that I was pressing onto the wrong side of the lighter.

I pressed down onto the lighter, holding the cigarette in my mouth, and that's how *I lit my first and what I thought would be my last cigarette.*

41

THE KICK (DOWN)

"Hey...hey, you okay?"

He patted my back as I coughed miserably and continuously. It felt like my throat, my lungs, my entire body, was trying to resent what I was taking in. It felt like it wasn't my cigarette that was on fire, but my heart. I could literally feel my heart burn.

"What is this shit? oh my God!" I shouted.

He calmly replied, "You'll get used to it, just...calm down," as he smoked his own cigarette.

"That's what you said, it's supposed to do, calm me down...but it didn't!" I continued to cough, as my words were barely clear and audible due to all the dry cough that was building up, "I can barely breathe Ansh!"

"Okay. Okay. Just wait a minute. I should have told you this before...you're not supposed to take a long puff, or too much smoke in one go. That's probably the reason why you're turning pale, green and coughing like a maniac..."

I screamed at him, "O my God! what do I do?"

He shouted over my voice, "Do you want to look cool or not?"

"I do!"

He continued to shout even louder, as though trying to make a chant out of it. "Do you want to make friends or not?"

"I f*cking do!"

He asked the final question, shouting even louder, that triggered me, "Do you want to forget whatever happened back at home or not?"

"Yes, yes yes I do!" I screamed back at him.

He grabbed me by the arms, trying to calm me down, "Fine Sana, then bare it. It's just the first time. Just take a few more puffs, and *I promise you*, if you don't feel legit in heaven, I'll call this party off."

I don't know what I thought, maybe it was the curiosity of...knowing what heaven feels like. Or maybe, it was the desire to try new things again and again, or maybe it was just that he was persuasive enough, and I really did want to forget everything that happened at home, and I was perhaps too desperate for an up class social life, that I decided to take a few more puffs, thinking this to be the only respite.

"Yes! That's the spirit! You just can't simply give up, right?"

"Yeah okay."

"Now listen up. You take the smoke into your mouth, and hold it in there for a while. Don't just take it all in...otherwise it'll be a repeat of what happened a few minutes ago. Then, you take out the cigarette, and inhale the smoke into your lungs. After like a few seconds, blow the smoke out through your mouth or your nose...but the nose is more for pros like me. Then you tap away the ash, and as your cigarette reaches the butt, you keep it away. Got it?"

"Got it, yeah."

The cigarette was once again lying in between my lips, ready to be used. I pulled in some smoke into my mouth, and did as he told, I tried to exhale through my mouth first, and as I did, I coughed more again. I realized that my cheeks were getting red and hot, while my skin was getting pale. I continued to cough, but I also continued to think about everything that God had been doing to me recently.

I thought about Papa, I thought about Natasha, I thought about the stupid fights I kept getting into. I thought about how, even after I did everything right, I got into trouble. I thought about my good grades, my improved swimming style, and most importantly, I thought about how in the past few days, the only good thing that has actually happened with me was me qualifying for districts, and that too was about to be taken away from me. And I just couldn't take it. So, I continued to smoke that damn cigarette.

And just when my very first cigarette was about to finish, *I felt it*.

The kick.

Relaxing.

Like the purest moment of joy.

Almost like a new life beginning.

Like all my troubles are melting away.

I felt light.

So full of life.

As I closed my eyes, I could tell I was on zenith.

I could feel all my worries, my sorrows, my troubles, melt away; or perhaps I could feel them turn into ash and smoke. It was like I was inhaling this intoxicating air, that was changing all my problems into smoke, that my body exhaled. With every puff I took, I could feel myself get lighter, and lighter.

It was like I had reached my ultimate goal of true happiness, joy and fulfillment. After all, isn't that exactly what we all crave for? What we all fight for? What we all live for? And I was getting all that in that one little cigarette.

I couldn't let it go.

The crystal glass which was placed alongside which the box of insignia on the wooden table inside the cabana caught my eyes, and I got glimpse of myself.

A cigarette stuck between the fingers, dull grey-cloudy shaped smoke escaped my seemingly-thin lips. My cheeks were oddly warmed, while my eyes seemed rather dim, a hand rested on my shoulder, which belonged to Ansh.

The slow wind gentle swooshed my hair, and making the burning cigarette's rims glow.

The Burning Truth

As I reflected in the crystals of the glass, I saw someone who I failed to recognize. I saw someone who people look up to. Someone who people want to personally know. Someone who would be included, someone who would be mature and cool. Someone who was the opposite of who Sana Sharma was.

❀ ❀ ❀

But before I knew it, the cigarette was over. I opened my eyes, and looked around. The music was still blaring, and the place was still filled with people. I was still at the same party, I had reached no heaven. Then I saw it lying there once again, the same black matte box, with eighteen more passes to heaven, and I couldn't resist the urge. "*Just one more,*" I asked.

Section 2

THE DESCENT

42

FLASHBACKS

I could hear someone banging on the door. Although I was quite used to this, that morning, as I lay in bed, the banging on the door seemed more like someone was beating the drums right on my ears. It was screeching and it was painful.

"Stop banging the door!" I screamed as loud as I could, but it came out more like a whisper.

"Sana, I'm coming in." said an excruciatingly loud voice which resembled Mummas.'

"Yeah okay. Just stop shouting for heaven's sake!" I tried to shout back again, but no voice really escaped my throat.

As I fluttered my eyes, I caught sight of Mumma who had barged into the room, and was now opening the curtains, from where an agonizingly plenty amount of sunlight was falling onto my room floor, whilst lighting up the entire room.

That's when my already exhausted brain started to work a little, and I realized, what was happening, where I was, and what time of the day it was, the only thing that I couldn't really manage to remember that well was, *how did I end up there?*

After Mumma pulled the curtains aside, she tied them together with the curtain pull backs. She then opened the door to my room, and so I could clearly hear the sound of the pressure cooker whistle from the kitchen, to me it sounded more like a rusty mini steam engine at work.

She then came and sat next to me, on my bed. I tried to pull myself up from the sleeping position into a sitting position, but I still felt nauseous and my head was spinning faster than a merry-go-round. My hands were cold, and I could tell that my face was a little pale, or perhaps even green.

I looked at Mumma who was perhaps waiting for an explanation for why I am still wearing the dress that I wore to the party, or why I am waking up when more than half the day is over, at 2 pm. Or maybe she simply wants to know what the hell had happened last night. And sadly, I had no answer to all these questions.

"So...are you going to say something? Any justification?" She questioned, and paused. "*Anything at all?*" She continued sarcastically.

She looked at me, with her eyes full of hope, she was perhaps hoping that I'd still have a logical explanation for all that happened. Her eyelids dropped, and her smile faded away.

"I don't remember exactly Mumma..." I tried to speak, and as I did, I coughed and it felt like things were coming back to me. "I remember stomping out of this place, and taking an Uber to reach Rixton, there I saw Papa's message which said um...something about how he's..." I almost choked on the word, "*ashamed*...of me."

"Yeah, okay. Then?" She asked impatiently.

"Then...I have this vivid memory...we were at the party. I was really sad, it was as if there were...so many people, you know? And no one, not a single one wanted to talk to me." I continued to cough a little. "Plus, Papa's message...it made me so sad."

"What happened afterwards?" She gave me the look she did when she already knew something, but just wanted to hear it from my mouth. But, for some reason, I could tell she didn't know everything, and neither did I.

"Well, Ansh, the guy whose birthday it was, found me, we ended up talking, and he umm...gave me tips on how to make friends..." I murmured, "and stuff like that. That's all that happened, I guess."

There was complete silence for some time.

She squinted her eyes, and leered towards me. Her brows snapped together, and her lips faked a smile. "So, that's all you remember?"

I muffled, "Yeah...I mean, I guess so..."

She pursed her lips together, seeming like she was still hoping for a better explanation or justification. When I failed to say anything about the smoking part, which I did remember after all, she finally decided to speak.

"Now, hear my side of the story. It was 7 am in the morning, your father was still, extremely angry from the other night. Co-incidentally, the minute he exited the main door to our house, I got a call from the front desk at Rixton."

Oh shit.

She continued bluntly, "They told me that when they were cleaning up the swimming arena in the morning, they found you on the floor in the corner of the area, clutching the rod to the speakers tightly."

Oh crap.

"I was then told, to please come and pick up my daughter who was almost wrecked, and unable to wake up, because she had passed out from the night before." She spoke brusquely.

Oh my God.

"So, I drove all the way to The Rixton, for my daughter who was on the verge of collapsing, and got her back home. Can you imagine how scared I was when they said, *unable to wake up?* Can you imagine my condition when they said you had *passed out?* Do you have any clue what happened after you left? Do you realize what you put me through? What you put *yourself* through? Can you imagine how traumatized I was?" She was now shouting, "*Do you get me? Do you, really?*"

Oh my God!

43

GROUNDED?

"Mumma, I'm sorry. I...I really don't know how I ended up here."

I took a deep breath, and I shrugged my shoulders as I began, "I really have no clue." I was lying, I knew. But I thought, it's better to skip out on the little bit of information that I still remembered, because telling her would only traumatize her even more.

"Oh God, just...just don't apologize now. It's not...Just leave it. And go take a shower. You smell like a gutter. We'll sort this out once you're done." Her tone was a mix of sadness and anger. I couldn't differentiate, it was perhaps the sadness that her stellar child ended up like this, and the anger about how she let me end up like this.

As she stomped out of the room, shutting the door behind her, I was certain that I had never seen her in a mood like this. And I didn't want to see her again like that either.

As the drops of water slid over my bare body, I forced my eyes shut, and I tried to rewind the sequence of events from the night before, and it all started to come back in flashes.

A clear image of me smoking a cigarette with Ansh popped up in my head. Then I recalled taking a few more of them from the...black box. For a second, I couldn't remember what happened next, but then as I scrubbed my body, trying to remove the disgusting smell that was stuck to it, another vivid image popped up.

I remembered standing in front of that bitch... Natasha. I was standing opposite her, with a cigarette in my mouth. I recollected her saying something on the lines of, "Are you sucking on a lollipop loser?" And I don't exactly remember what happened later...but somehow, I managed to impress them, and she said something like... "Oh, you smoke?" And then, I recalled sitting with her, next to her. With all of them...something like that.

For some reason, I couldn't think of what happened after that, but whatever it was, I knew that I had finally made friends with Natasha and her gang. Ultimately, I had won and made some friends at Avenues. My low, sucking social life was actually over, it was a new life, a new beginning, at least that's what I thought at that time.

We were both sitting on the dining table, opposite to one another. This was the first time because Mumma always sat next to me, not opposite to me. She didn't make eye contact for the majority of our lunch time but when she finally did, she said something she had never said before, "You're grounded."

And as she said this, she picked up her plate, pushed in her chair, and headed straight to the kitchen. She did not wait a second for me to even respond. She just took the decision, with no discussion. *This was not her way of handling things! How could she do that?*

As she walked towards her room, I shouted from the dining table, "For how long?"

She turned around, and looked at me, but not directly. She was actually looking at the wall behind me, I could tell. "Forever? Or at least till the districts."

"But that's over a month!"

"For what you did yesterday, you should be grounded for your lifetime. No discussion on this Sana." she said as she shut the door close to her room, right on my face, I could even clearly hear the lock turn, and make a click noise from the inside.

"But that's not your way!" I shouted, so that my voice reached the other end of the door. But there was no reply.

I had never seen her this angry.

When I went back to my room, I thought about what had happened, everything that had happened in the past few hours. It all started to cloud my mind, the screaming, the shouting, Papa, Mumma, the party, the message, my life basically, what it was *before* and what it was *now*.

As I thought more and more about it, the thought that I am stuck inside this house for at least a month, the fact that my father might not even talk to me for the rest of my life, the idea of Mumma, my best friend, being angry at me, all just for making friends, it was killing me. I could feel my ears get hot, and my eyes pop out.

And for some odd reason, I thought about all of it, I felt this urge, this strong desire, craving and longing for something to cool me off. Something that would just, take me away for a while, help me escape reality. So, I decided to do what I generally did whenever I was pissed off, put on some music on my beats headphones.

When I turned on my playlist the first song that came up was 'Closer,' by The Chainsmokers, UGHHH. It was hurting my ears. I tried to shut it off, but my hands were shaking so much, that I ended up increasing the volume.

I flung my headphones at the wall. They crashed and collapsed on the floor.

It felt like the entire night was coming back to me. Why did I end up in trash? Why did I end up smelling like gutter? Then, after all those bad things clogged the drain of my mind, I suddenly thought of that paradise like feeling that I got after my first cigarette.

That's when I realized, I was craving for the same feeling, the relief, the joy, the calmness that followed it.

44

APOLOGY ACCEPTED?

It was Monday morning, and I hadn't had a chance to see Papa since the last Friday night. I knew he was in town because I saw his things lying around, I heard his voice through the walls late at night, when I couldn't sleep thinking about everything that happened. He was either avoiding and ignoring me or, he was just busy with work. I hoped it was the latter.

Now, it was my turn to finally face Mumma; ever since she had grounded me, we had not spoken directly. She mostly used sentences like "Go sleep" and "Go eat." (Since, I hadn't really yet had a proper talk with Papa, I decided it's better if I just continue with swimming). Mumma was the one who drove me for my morning swimming practice, she had no other choice but to spend the next thirty-five minutes, to school, sitting next to me in a closed car.

As we got into the car, I could tell mumma was unhappy that she had to drive me to school.

"Mumma, can we talk about this weekend?"

"No." She replied.

"Please?"

"What is even left to talk about?"

"Look I just...want to apologize."

"For what Sana? For what?"

"For everything. For bailing out on you, and leaving you all alone with Papa, for ending up like I did, at Rixton, for making you feel any less... because of me." A solemn tear escaped the corner of my eyes and dropped on my school bag. "I'm sorry Mumma. I really am."

She let out a sigh and shook her head. I couldn't tell what she was thinking, but I was hoping she understood what I was trying to say.

For a long while she remained silent, so, I decided to further give justification for myself. "I just wanted to make friends...live a life like I did in FPS. I didn't want to end up in trouble." I tried to fight the tears that were building up, waiting to pour down, "I'm sorry Mumma. Please talk to me at least once! I didn't want things to end like this."

"It's okay." She replied bluntly.

I could tell she didn't mean it. She probably said so, to simply shut me up. Why would she do that?

"Mumma, I really am sorry, why don't you understand?"

She pushed down the brakes, and the car came to a quick halt. We were just about to enter the school premises. On reaching the gate I could tell that the guards at the entrance were staring at us.

"Fine. Let's get this sorted for once and for all. "She paused, and then continued, "What do I not understand?" She shook her head in horizontal motion, with disappointment, "Do I not understand that my daughter was in garbage condition when I got her back home? Or that *my* daughter, who I gave birth to, is now so *big* that she didn't even consider it important to reply to all the messages *I* sent. Tell me, *what do I not understand Sana?*"

My lashes fluttered, as I tried to hold back my tears, but they started to come out one after the other, I couldn't look at her anymore. I knew if I wanted to get out of my mental agony condition, I needed to tell her the truth. So, I looked away, outside my window, and stared at a board that read, 'We is the English Mastery, English Guroo – For professionals.'

I made no eye contact with her for my eyes would have said too much, "Mumma, you don't understand... what it's like to have almost zero friends in a gigantic school like Avenues, just because of some silly incident that happened with a girl, who rules Middle School. You don't understand, what it's like knowing that your dream, of swimming, is about to be snatched from your hands, and you have no clue about what it's like having your father say, "he's ashamed of you" even after you do everything right."

She still had her hands firmly placed on the steering wheel, but her eyes looked away, and I didn't know where we were headed with this conversation, but I once again started to feel that urge, that desire to calm down, however, this time, I felt that I *needed* it to relax before my head bursts.

She released the brakes, and our car started to move towards the school building. We finally reached our destination, and she still hadn't responded to what I had said. Although we had reached the parking area, where I always got down, instead of getting off the car; I waited inside, waiting for her to reply. After a minute, she finally responded.

"I know you smoked that day, and probably drank too. And I get it. You had a lot of pressure...stress, and a lot of things. But till the time it doesn't happen again, it's fine."

I knew she'd understand, after all, she was my Mumma, she knew me, inside and out.

"Thank you Mumma, I love you so much."

"Okay, but you're still grounded until districts."

I couldn't get this. One moment she says it's okay, it's fine. But then she said I'm still grounded till districts. *How does that even make sense?* But, I didn't want to aggravate the situation further in the car, and in my head even more, so, I got down, smiled, and went away.

As I walked towards the swimming arena, after all the drama in the car and the horrifying weekend that kept playing on rewind in my mind, I knew I needed a cigarette. I needed it so badly, the only question was, *how do I get it*, if I'm grounded?

45

-CRAVINGS-

During our morning practice, we were working on my six-beat kick. And as I did, I could think about how the first time my coaches had told me all these terms, and I had freaked out so much. Now it made all made sense I not only knew what these seemingly complex words meant, I also knew how to do this stuff in reality; and now that I did, Papa might snatch it away from me.

It was like giving a child a lollipop, and as soon as they start to eat it, you snatch the lollipop without any reason.

I was lost in my thoughts when Ms. Yadav shouted from outside the water, "Adopting the 6-beat kick will make conserving your legs easier and increase your stroke efficiency when it comes to racing, even if you race with this technique or not."

I continued to count, "One-two-three—one-two-three" or "Right-two-three—left-two-three" in my head, trying to keep track of me legs, just like in waltz.

That day, during swimming practice, I tried so hard, to remove that craving for a cigarette from my head,

The Burning Truth

trying to enjoy the water like I always did, but all I could think about was about me being still grounded, and how Papa might ruin my just beginning swimming career.

Soon, it got worse. As we headed towards the changing rooms, Ms. Yadav called out from behind, "Just a reminder for you guys, we'll be calling your parents either today or tomorrow, to talk about additional classes outside school, alright?"

Everyone nodded, and went to change, but I was terrified. I knew what the result would be if they ended up calling Papa and telling him about the additional coaching. He'd probably, no, he'd *definitely* tell Ms. Yadav or Mr. Jain that he does not approve of all this, and that I should be working on my academics not some mere competition. It would be the perfect opportunity for him to destroy everything for me.

I needed a cigarette.

❁ ❁ ❁

Ever since I joined swimming, my speed had increased and so had my stamina. That day, when I rushed up the stairs to find Ansh, I did not end up stopping after every three or four stairs, neither did I take ten minutes to climb three flights of stairs, in fact I was quite swift while rushing up the stairs.

If I was grounded for a month, it meant I couldn't go out to buy a cigarette, which I was determined to make my last. So, I knew if I had any hope of getting another cigarette, it's through Ansh. Once I reached our floor, my feet paced towards Ansh's form room, but he wasn't there.

According to my watch, I had exactly six minutes to find Ansh and get a cigarette from him before the school starts. So, I rushed to the lockers, but he wasn't there either.

My eyes scanned the area, but he was nowhere in the corridors either. That's when it clicked, I recalled a place where I had previously seen Natasha and her gang sitting and smoking, and with her, I had seen Ansh. In a school as big as Avenues, it was a small little corner. I had seen them sitting on the steps that were outside the isolated store room building. According to Dev, my buddy who I had now started to talk a lot to, they sat there because these steps directly connected one to the kitchen of the dining hall through some hidden passage which made it a safe spot.

Without wasting another second, I went out of the school building, ran across the gigantic field and towards the store room. After a few minutes of jogging, I could see their body outlines in the far distance. I could tell they were all sitting in a group, and apart from them, there was no one around. I thought about what I was about to do. I knew that they always said, if you pick up the second cigarette, you're done. But, then I thought about how Papa would take away my dream from me today, and I just knew that I needed a puff or two.

As I took a step towards them, I thought, *just one last time.*

Sitting there on the steps that led to the store was Natasha, and her friends. If one were to look at them in that minute, they'd say she's trying to replicate a scene from Gossip Girl where she's Blair Waldorf, aka Queen

B, whose seated right at the top of the steps, followed by her minions who were sitting below her and then right towards the end were a couple of guys which thankfully included Ansh Roy.

Even though I vaguely remembered sitting with Natasha, or something of that sort, I didn't precisely have a clue of what actually happened that night, and I didn't really trust the few flashbacks and memories I had. I was confused and wondered *did I really sit with them, and if I did, did I also party with them?* I knew that by asking them themselves, I would end up making a fool of myself.

The only person who I thought could actually tell me what happened that night was Ansh, but I didn't have the time for that. At that moment, all I wanted were a few puffs to energize me and calm my mind. Hence, I tried to make minimal eye contact with anyone else sitting on the steps, and tried to climb my way down the stairs towards Ansh as quickly as possible.

As I walked down the steps towards him, I could feel all the pairs of eyes staring at me, it was like my first day all over again. No one said anything, they just followed me with their eyes, and passed random smirks to one another. It felt like I was in this unknown, dangerous, Natasha-dominated territory.

Two girls who I recalled from seeing on the day of my economics test, were judging me from top-to bottom as I cross their step. Then there was Dev, my buddy as well. He passed me a vivid smile, that seemed filled with jealousy for some reason and then right at the end, I could see Ansh smiling at me, and as I came towards him, he stood up with a questioning expression. Since he wasn't giving his usual all-teeth-exposed smile, I pulled his arm, and took him aside towards the dining hall.

His eyebrows waggled, in an interrogative manner. "Is everything okay?" He asked. And before I could reply, he added, "By the way, you were amazing the other night."

Amazing my ass!

I tried to calm myself down. Amazing? That night has ruined my life, I had thought that I'd simply dress well, make an impression and make some friends and come back home. That night was a disaster and he was a part of it. *Why did he have to make me try that cigarette*, what was the point? UGHHH

"Look, we need to talk about what happened the other night...but right now..." I looked at my watch and told him, "we just have about a minute and a half before class begins, so I need a small...favor from you."

"What is–"

He didn't get to answer my question, leave alone give me a cigarette because Natasha called out to both of us from the steps.

"What is it Ansh? Can we help in anyway?"

Wait. *Was Natasha trying to help me?* Is everything all right with her? What was even happening? And that's when it hit me, maybe it's because of the other night, maybe I actually did make friends with her...

He held me by my wrist gently and took me in front of her, and I gave her the death stare, that said, "what's wrong with you both, let go of me."

Before I knew it, he blabbered, "Natz, Sana needs a favor...That's all."

I looked at her, and blinked my eyes.

She raised a brow, and announced, "Guys listen up!" She clapped, in a rhythmic fashion, trying to get the attention (which she already had). "Sana is now our friend, whatever help she needs, we'd give."

How did mortal enemies become friends?

46

MY NEW FRIENDS :)

"So...what is it Sana?" Ansh asked politely.

Now, I did not want to make a big deal out of this whole thing. Obviously. Why would I spoil my perfectly good reputation (not really) where I'm seen as a good girl? Why couldn't I just do this in private?

I nudged Ansh, trying to indicate to him that let's go to a corner. But for some reason, it seemed like he purposely failed to understand what I was trying to say.

She tilted her head, like Barbie, as she said, "Sana, is it something you can't tell your *friends?*"

Multiple thoughts clouded my judgement, *what if I told her and she told a teacher or something? What if she records me taking a cigarette and posts it on social media? What if she simply embarrasses me by making fun of how I thought she was a friend of mine?* What if this and what if that? That's when I looked at my watch and saw that we barely had a few seconds before the bell rang. Although Ms. Sehgal was pretty chilled, I didn't want to be late. So, I came clean.

The Burning Truth

"I need a cigarette."

"A *cigarette...*" she said in an interrogative tone.

I simply nodded.

"You...don't have your own dealer or source or something?"

"Oh um...no. I just a needed this one cigarette, not like a box or anything of that –"

"Don't worry, you've got it."

She turned around at an angle of around 160 degrees, to grab her bag. She put her hand inside the front pocket, and took out a box of gold flakes. She wrapped her hand around it, as though making it feel warm, she stared at it for a mere second and then passed it on.

I was amazed that I remembered what Ansh had told me that night about always shaking an opened box, so I did the same. Then I unwrapped the transparent cover and flipped open the box. Out came a cigarette, and I slipped it into my pocket. I placed the leftover cigarettes that were in the box, on my palm and tried to return it to Natasha.

"Here you go, and umm...thanks a ton."

"Oh Sana, stop with the thanks. And please keep the box."

Why was she being so nice? Anyway, I didn't want the box, because I was determined that I'd take only a single cigarette, which would be my last.

"No um...that's really nice of you, but I just need one." I told her hesitantly

She gritted her teeth as she replied, "Just keep it."

I insisted, "Look I just, need one. I don't smoke that often."

She blinked her eyes in slow motion, as though trying to prove her point. "Consider it a return gift from Ansh for his birthday, okay Sana?"

I could tell she was getting pissed, and I didn't want to end up in a fight again, with my new 'friend' so, I grasped the box and tried to hide it in my pocket.

"Thanks again Natasha...and Ansh; I'll uh...see you guys later."

Ansh said bye like a normal human being, but Natasha did her famous 'wave wave' where she waved at anyone who was going away or coming towards her, but the special thing was that she waved her fingers like the ocean waves. To me, it was plain creepy, but to some people it was the only thing that mattered.

PS. Many girls at Avenues even tried to copy her move, and it looked even more ridiculous than when Natasha did it.

But as she did this wave I realized, she only did it to her very close friends, so, maybe she was actually serious. Maybe she did mean whatever she said. Perhaps that party wasn't that bad after all. I mean, at least some good came out of it.

That day at school, I remained completely distracted. Not because I basically had a time bomb in my bag (the box of cigarettes) which if found, could possibly get me rusticated. That wasn't the only thing. I was also thinking about the call from Ms. Yadav to Papa, and how I had no clue or control on my life, whatsoever.

47

THE LAST CIGARETTE

As soon as I got home, I went to *the Mandir* to grab a matchbox as I had never used a cigarette lighter, but I ended up ransacking the entire place, till I found a small matchbox with a few matchsticks and they worked.

Now, all I needed was my cigarette and a place where I could smoke. I could've gone outside and that would've been my safest bet, but I'm grounded. Then I thought, what if Mumma told me to go outside *herself*? Perhaps for groceries or something?

So, I went to Mumma's door and knocked on it. When she opened the door, her hair was all over her face, and her eyes seemed red, it seemed like she had been crying, but I was too afraid to ask her why? She didn't greet me with her regular smile. Nevertheless, I still decided to ask her.

"Do you need any groceries or anything Mumma? Anything from the Foods Mart or Daily Needs?"

She gave a me blank expression and softly said, "No, not really. Why?"

"Well, just like that...I thought it would be nice if I could be of some help to you."

For a second she seemed suspicious, because never in my entire life have I asked Mumma, if she needs my help with home stuff. But, I think she probably bought it, thinking that I am trying to clean up all the mess between us by doing these small things.

"You can go and uh...get two liters of milk, that's all I guess."

"Okay sure." I said, while trying to control the smile over my face.

After she handed me some money, I headed straight to my room, grabbed my sling, put in the cigs and the matchsticks, plus, the money and got out of the house immediately.

I started to walk on the ceramic-textured road, towards the store; it was only when I saw that our house is completely out of sight, when I finally took out that one cigarette, which I was sure would be my last.

I chose a spot to sit, it was close to the store, and yet far away. Most people neglected the spot where I was sitting because it had a rather strange smell to it, due to the washroom that it was next to it. Before I pressed the cig against my lips, I thought of how Papa was going to probably debar me from even going to the washroom when I meet him after this. And that was all I needed to convince myself that yes, *I needed this god damn cigarette.*

I lit the cigarette and took a long puff, it filled my lungs, then I could feel it travel back towards my mouth.

My mouth opened, for letting the smoke out spontaneously. I took another puff, this time releasing the smoke through my nose. And I realized it did look cool actually, and it was also so much more relaxing.

After a few minutes, I was feeling so light, lighter than air, calmer than the ocean, more relaxed than a newborn baby. But for some reason, it didn't feel enough. It didn't feel as good as the last time. Or maybe I was just exaggerating my last experience in my thoughts. I mean although the cigarette brand is different, *it doesn't really matter, does it?*

I went inside the store at last and purchased milk as told, that's when I discerned, Mumma would instantly get to know I smoked, if I go home like this, so, I took a box of the strongest mints they had, from my own money. That leaves me with twelve rupees from my pocket money. It hit me, *smoking is bloody expensive!*

As I got out of the store, I saw the cigarette I had put out a few minutes back, and I felt the craving to take another one. I knew my brain was just desiring the same kind of heavenly feeling like it felt the other night, and todays wasn't just equally pleasing. So, I decided to smoke another last one, to satisfy myself.

I sat there outside, towards the back of the store, and smoked another cigarette, and thankfully, by then, I actually felt better. The smoke enveloped me in its own magical bubble, and for a brief moment I forgot about all that had happened or were about to happen. I wish that bubble, where people are always happy, could last forever.

Before I rang the bell to our front door, I took out my handkerchief and wiped my lips, my hands and even brushed away my clothes, in case some ash may have fallen on them. Then, I took out another mint, just to be double sure, to rub away the smell from me.

I finally rang the bell, and thankfully, our helper came to open the door, before she could say anything much, I kept everything on the dining table and headed straight to my room. I put on as much of perfume as possible, and then looked at myself in the mirror. I looked just the same, I thought.

When Papa came home, I was prepared. Prepared for a long ass lecture and a good shout or so, but usually things don't always turn out the way you expect them to.

We were all sitting on the dining table, quietly. On a regular day, if there was a chance when Papa figured out some time to *actually* have dinner with us, I'd tell Mumma and him about my whole day. But today, it was just not the same.

He told me to pass the rice, and as I did, he said with food in his mouth, "So, your umm...swimming instructor had called me today. She was talking about how you'll need an extra coach...because the districts are very close, and there's less time left."

I blinked my eyes rapidly, and nodded simultaneously. How else was I supposed to respond after all?

He calmly continued, "I told her that we'd look for an instructor immediately and get you enrolled."

WHAT? Was this some kind of a joke? What was happening?

The Burning Truth

Wrinkles of surprise appeared on my head, and my heart started to pound like a train rushing on the tracks. I had no clue what was happening, and how it was happening.

Mumma picked up her plate, and went towards the kitchen, even though her food was unfinished. It seemed that she had done this on purpose so that Papa and I could talk one on one. (Although our kitchen wasn't exactly closed, so she could pretty much see and hear everything that was happening).

"I don't get what's happening..."

"Look, I might have come out not the way you were probably hoping, the last time. But the thing is..." He pressed his lips together, as though his body was resisting him from telling me whatever he wished to say. After a pause, he continued, "my father...your grandfather, always told me to focus on my academics. But I never really listened to him, and went along with my music. A thing I loved and lived for, I was meant for it."

A single drop of guilt surged up from the corner of his eye, as he continued to tell, "I thought I would just walk up to any music competition, ace it, make money and the end. But you know that didn't happen. I ended up failing as a musician. Then, I had to redo my college years, and that just...messed up my entire life plan. When I finally got through college, I got a job in the corporate world, a place where I could barely imagine myself being a few years ago."

I knew what he was saying, I now understood why all my life, all he wanted was for me to not repeat the same mistake. But then...

"So...what changed your mind Papa?" I questioned him in a soft voice.

He raised an eyebrow, and replied, "Well, the first thing your teacher said when I answered the phone was... Sana is one of our best swimmers, and we have high expectations from her. And I just thought...so what if *I* failed, it doesn't mean my daughter would fail too, right?"

"Right Papa" I tried, to resist the tears of happiness.

"Just don't let me down, or my belief shattered, okay? I'm trusting you."

I hugged him tight, and although I could not recall the last time he made any physical contact with me, that day, he did. He put both his arms around me, and clenched his palms together, making a human blanket around me. I saw Mumma walk over to her room, smiling at both of us.

When he finally let go of me, his eyes were glistening with pride, and mine with sudden father love. I had never seen him under this light, never knew he had a softer side to his dark, rocky personality. I wished to freeze that moment, and just let it be like that for the rest of eternity, and if I could, I would.

But, the show must go on.

48

SMOKING AND BONDING

The first thing I decided to do was to throw away that box of cigarettes gifted to me by Natasha. I knew that if I'd keep it, I'll probably crave for another cigarette, and another and another (at least that's what I had been told by endless smokers). So, I slipped the box that was half full of cigarettes into my bag, waved my now-happy parents goodbye, and started to walk towards the bus stop.

A few meters away from me, my eyes spotted a large, dark green colored dustbin placed onto my left side. I turned around to ensure that mumma and papa had both returned to the house, and when I realized they were gone, for some odd reason, I thought, perhaps one last cigarette before I throw the box away would not make me addicted. So, I took out another cigarette directly from the box using my lips, lit it there, and smoked it, waiting for the bus to come.

A few minutes passed, and the bus had still not arrived. So, I thought that it was now time to let go of the few cigarettes that I was left with. I stood there by the dustbin, holding onto the box of gold flakes halfway inside the dustbin, when my mind got clogged with multiple thoughts.

The thoughts were of how this cig had got me through so many things, like the Papa crisis, or how it had helped me in various situations, like making friends with Natasha or just gaining some social acceptance (yes people actually knew me now, they didn't call me by 'new girl' but actually used my name, all probably because I sometimes hung around with Natasha and her group). It had most importantly, helped me find my position, my personality at Avenues International.

The bus rolled in, and started to blow the horn, signaling for me to hop onto the bus, but I couldn't let go of it.

I waited there, contemplating my next move, and somehow, my instincts directed me to keep that box of cigarette back into my bag, and run towards the bus, since it had already started to move ahead in slow-motion.

And that's when I knew, *I was hooked.*

Since a few days had gone by since Natasha or as I had started to call her now, 'Natz' had declared her sudden love towards me as a friend, I expected for us to bond more. But apart from hanging around in the corridors, exchanging a few smiles and waves here and there...we didn't really communicate much.

It was breakfast time, when Natz and her minions started to walk towards me in their rhythmic fashion. Suddenly a memory flashed in front of my eyes from when I had scored well in Economics, and they had come and humiliated me in front of the entire Middle

The Burning Truth

School. I started to think if I had recently done anything similar to deserve this again, but couldn't recollect anything because I, for some odd reason weren't doing that well.

They all stood at about a double-hand distance from me, and then Natz took a step closer as if to forming a triangle, just like she had done the last time. My heart pounded faster, and my hands started to sweat, I could feel my nerves pop out, and my pupils grow larger.

She flicked her hair and gave me her snooty smile, "Hey Sana! How are you?"

That's what she wanted to ask me? I hesitantly replied, "Umm...I am–"

I was interrupted, "Who am I kidding? I don't really care!" While I thought it was simply rude, she laughed it out, and her minions joined in.

No reply escaped my mouth this time.

She continued, "Now that we're friends, I'd like to officially invite you to our morning sessions by the steps. I hope to see you there tomorrow."

So that's what they were called. *Morning sessions...by the steps.* That's what was happening when I had gone to find Ansh for a cigarette and she gave me a whole pack.

My body couldn't digest the fact that I was officially invited for the morning session by Natasha herself. *I mean it was a big deal*, I thought. I graciously accepted her invitation and rushed to the washroom, to express my happiness in the cubicle, for I didn't want to convey that I was too desperate and overly joyed.

The next morning, right after my morning practice, I went straight up to the steps outside the dining room. When I reached their, a friend of Ansh, who was dressed shabbily, with shoe laces open, hair ruffled and a loose tie, shouted, "There's our newest member!" in a jovial tone, and I started to blush. Natasha was seated in her usual spot, right at the top of the pyramid. She did her wave-wave and welcomed me to the steps. It all seemed surreal to me.

The only step that was empty, was the last one, right at the bottom of the steps. And...there was some space next to Natz of course. But then, I couldn't sit next to her, due to obvious reasons. So, I took a seat on the last step. When I had thought about what happened in these sessions, I had imagined them gossiping about who's dating who. Who are they planning to humiliate next? Who is going to be the next victim? And stuff like that. Basically, the kind of topics we talked about at FPS during our gang meetings.

But instead, here's how *this one* went down:

Natz pointed at me using her index finger, and then signaled me to come and sit next to her. Yes, *next to her*.

Then, everyone took out a pack of cigs from their bags, most of them had gold flakes, I tried to follow along and so, I took out the same box which Natz had donated to me (*thank God, I didn't throw it*). She looked at me as though I have committed a great crime.

Her eye twitched, as she said in a sassy tone, "You are yet to finish that one box...from the other day?"

"Well...I don't really smoke that often actually. So, yeah." I didn't want to commit that I was trying to stay away, because you knew that could act as a barrier for our friendship.

"Oh sweetheart, were you saving for the future or something?" she asked me, while clutching my hand in a consoling manner.

"No not really..." I said uncomfortably due to the touching.

Before I knew it, she took out about four or five more boxes of mixed brands of cigarettes including gold flakes and insignia, and put them into the front zip of my bag.

"Just keep them, we smoke here every day, and if you smoke... say at least six or seven cigarettes daily, then these would probably last around a month. So, I guess you're covered."

This time, I didn't resist her offer. The reason this time was not just because I was scared, or because I thought she might eat me alive if I said no, but instead, deep down, it felt like I was now getting lured by the cigarette and hoping for this to happen.

Each of us took out a cig and lit it up.

We talked about the teachers, we talked about the students, we talked about the real stuff, *we gossiped*. In most cases, I stayed silent because I didn't really have a clue about what was happening and who they were talking about.

But *when we smoked, we bonded.*

49

'HIDING & SMOKING'

"Where do you keep running off to?" inquired Ms. Yadav, with her eyebrows knitted, and her hands on her hips. I shook my head in disagreement, and softly mumbled, "No-Nowhere Ms. Yadav."

Though, I exactly knew where I was running off to. I had recently started to sit around with Natz's gang, *every morning*, by the steps and talk to them, while we smoked before school started.

Natz said it was a way to relax ourselves and our minds before we started the hectic routine of the day, at school.

"People meditate. People do yoga. People do god-knows-what. But what I do is far superior than all these...I smoke."

By then, I had made my mind to totally agree with her, it was kind of like my morning tea before work. It calmed me down, and prepared me to take on whatever came on my way, be it my falling grades, bad feedback from teachers or just about anything else.

The Burning Truth

Coming back to the point, to reach the steps on time, I had to change quickly and rush back up to where they sat and Ms. Yadav probably noticed that.

She blinked her eyes and took a deep breath before she spoke in a deep voice, "Look Sana, Although I may only be a coach to you, but for me, *all of you* are my children. And I can tell when something is wrong with my child. I have been noticing you, and lately...you have been acting strangely."

What did she mean by acting strangely?

"I'm sorry Ms. Yadav."

"See, I don't know what you are into, or who you have started to mingle with, but I do know, that you are not as focused and devoted as you seemed when you started to swim here at Avenues."

A. I knew that she was aware about me hanging around with Natz's gang. Everyone knew. She just didn't want to say it openly.

B. I was equally focused and devoted, in fact smoking had started to help me focus. Plus, I convinced myself that my (falling) grades did not reflect my intellectual capacity.

I nodded, in acceptance, even though I didn't really agree with what she was saying, just to get over with the conversation, so that I don't get late for the morning session. But Ms. Yadav would *just not stop rambling.*

"I want to remind you, that we are...or at least *were* hoping good results from you...so, just please...please come back to your senses and start working harder, the competition is in almost two weeks and I need a better timing from you."

I mocked, "*A better timing?*"

"Of course. And remember, just because your performance seems unaffected right now, it doesn't mean it'll stay that way forever. You might not be able to see the difference now, but you'll see it eventually."

I nodded vertically, and then bowed my head, to say "Yes Ma'am."

It seemed like she realized that I hardly cared about what she was saying, because her eyes suddenly drooped and her body wasn't quite that stiff anymore. She once again shook her head in disagreement and murmured, "You don't care, do you? Just go...wherever you want to go to Sana."

"I care, Ms. Yadav. I'll work harder. I promise"

Of course, I cared, I mean this was the only thing Papa had ever supported me on. Both Mumma and Papa were putting in so much effort for me too. But I also cared about my friendship with Natz. And so, I had to leave. Sometimes we have to just...*prioritize.*

These morning sessions by the steps may not seem that important to some, but in a matter of a few days they had become the key to my social life. Now, all I had to do was smoke a few cigs with them in the morning, bitch about the kids that passed by and simply agree with what Natz said. By doing all this, I got to sit with them during lunch (yes, no more lonely lunch time), I got to walk with someone during dispersal, I had someone to ask for notes or help, *I always had someone.* Not Natz necessarily, but at least someone from the group.

And that meant a lot.

The more I stayed with them, the more they taught me and educated me. For instance, I learnt one day from Dev, that "never smoke after lunch, otherwise the smell of the smoke lingers on, and then your parents might find out." He told me that it was based on his own personal experience and so I trusted him. Gradually, the calculator in my bag was replaced by a few boxes of mint and the geometry box was replaced with a bottle of perfume. And by now I had learnt the art of *smoking and hiding.*

We were all only getting closer, and it was a good feeling. I mean, for once, I felt wanted and needed, I felt a part of something, after so long...and I hadn't felt this way ever since I left FPS.

Dev, the person who had volunteered to become my buddy initially, had gradually become one of my best friends. This was because of the various common lessons we had, plus he was mutual friends with Natz, hence, we always sat together by the steps. Not only this, we were also in the same section, and the same swimming team which meant we had a lot of time on our hands together.

The only difference was that he didn't really smoke that much, while I had by then started to smoke at least six-seven cigs per day, he generally stayed away because of the *prolonged cough* issue he had. Nevertheless, we clicked on many things and the more I spent time with him, the more we got closer.

50

THE DREADFUL HEALTH CHECKUP

The next day was our health check-up.

"Dev, you're up next at the Dental station." Announced the nurse.

I waved him all the best as he walked towards the dental station that was equipped with stainless steel tools that seemed excruciatingly dangerous. He used hand gestures to indicate that he's dead, by curling his ring and pinkie finger inside, such to make a gun. We both chuckled a little as he did so.

Once he was gone, I looked around the infirmary. It wasn't much different than the one at FPS, but it was much larger, and cleaner. Also, at FPS we didn't really have a dentist *and* a general doctor. We only had a doctor who came once in a while, and a nurse who looked after everything else.

Before I could indulge in deeper thoughts, my name was called out. I was next.

The Burning Truth

I sat there on the reclined patient's seat that was covered in a weird sticky plastic like material. The dentist didn't waste much time on smiling or anything, she quickly pointed the big bright yellow light that was overhead, right towards my face, and used the mouth mirror to investigate the insides of my little mouth.

A few minutes had passed by, when I noticed her face grew serious and mysterious. Her eyes twitched a little and her voice mellowed down as she sighed and said, "You need professional cleaning, your teeth are becoming pale and icky."

Pale and icky? I always had a perfect dental hygiene record for a long time, so, how did this happen? I wondered.

"Umm…okay."

"This is either because you don't brush your teeth well, or you're consuming something that's turning them into this…. something like cigarettes."

It was an instant reaction to give false justification for myself, "Oh…um, I don't smoke. So, maybe I just need to brush better."

She replied brusquely, "I never said you smoke." I knew that if she wanted she could've called up my parents and all that, but it seemed like she barely cared as she continued, "nevertheless, you must consider getting them cleaned as soon as possible. Otherwise, this can lead to loss of teeth. Now off you go."

A sigh of relief escaped my mouth, but the first thought that came to my head was, what if she'd have found out? I'd probably get rusticated. But what came to my mind next was more horrifying, *was smoking actually taking a toll on my appearance? Were my teeth actually getting paler by the day?*

I was then headed towards the general physician, when she checked my weight, I realized that it had reduced a little. I felt brief happiness for a minute or two. Only to be spoilt when the doctor checked me for the baggy eyes that I had developed.

With knitted eyebrows, she inquired, "Do you not sleep at night? Is your sleeping pattern disturbed?"

How did she figure that out? I mean, it was true. I hadn't been able to sleep the way I did since the past few days because my mind often kept me awake wanting some more...craving some more...needing some more of that kick I got after smoking, but I couldn't smoke in the house. So, these days I often just lay in bed, sleepless, for hours.

I made something up, "Doctor my dog keeps barking, and I just can't sleep at night because of that."

Thankfully that made her drift off topic, as she said in aw, "You have a dog!? Which breed?"

Typical woman.

But the problem was *I knew nothing about dogs!* So, I tried to cover up, "It's umm...small. And fur-furry." However, by then I had lost her because she picked up my report, and began to write and talk simultaneously, "Okay...it's small and furry.... Is 'it' a he or a she?"

"Oh yeah, it's a he..."

She stopped writing, dropped the parker pen onto the board and looked up, "Okay, can I now see your nails please?"

I raised both my palms, inverted them, and showed my nails to her. My nails were perfectly trimmed, and that is why I was surprised when her eyes popped out, and her jaw dropped down to the floor.

"It seems like your hands are getting yellow and hands yellow...plus, the droopy eyes." She took a deep breath and claimed, "They are a sign of smoking..."

I was dead.

That's when I noticed my hands, they weren't exactly yellow because I hadn't been smoking for long, but they were getting yellow from the place where I held my cigarette.

An image of an old, yellow hand, with brittle and broken dirty nails that were falling off, came to my mind.

Why was this happening? Why was it happening at all? *What should I tell her? I couldn't get caught!*

"Doctor...I have no reason, to uh...smoke. I told you, the droopy eyes were thanks to my cute...dog. And this, I really don't know. I'll tell my mom and get it checked."

"Alright, but I am giving you only a month, otherwise, I'll call your mom and tell her about my observation."

"Yes Doctor."

Before she had the chance to say anything further, I made my way to the washroom. I shut myself in the dainty little cubicle and sat there on the pot, with my head in my palms. *How did it get so far?*

When I finally exited the washroom, Dev was standing there, waiting for me with his hands crossed across his chest.

"What happened Sana? I saw you running out of the infirmary."

I tried to shoo him away, "Nothing Dev. Let's go for the next lesson."

Before I could stop him, or even realize what was happening, he clutched me by the arm, and forced me to show me my hands to him. His face suddenly dimmed, and his eyes narrowed as he inspected my hands.

"Did the doc say anything about your hands? Them seem perfectly normal to me."

They didn't.

I failed to reply, while he continued, "You know you could've said something like...I was having *haldi* that's why my hands are like this, or something of that sort."

Why the hell did that not click my mind?

51

WHEN REALITY STRIKES

All I wanted to do was smoke a cigarette and forget everything that just happened at the infirmary, even though I knew, that the yellow teeth and hands and the sleepy eyes were all because of that cigarette.

That's when I thought, something is seriously wrong with me. I looked at my hands again and saw the patch that was getting a little yellow. The more I thought about it, the more I craved a cigarette, and it wasn't long before when I had managed to escape the school building, and was sitting outside, smoking a cig.

The next day, we were sitting down for lunch. Mumma was sitting opposite to me, and on the table, lay multiple food delicacies, some of which were my favorite. On a regular day, Mumma would cook, at most, one *sabzi* for main course, along with some sort of *daal*. But that day, there lay an entire three course buffet in front of me.

"What is all this?" I asked Mumma, gesturing at the food that lay ahead of me.

"It's food...food that you like." She replied softly, with a smile.

"Is everything alright...Mumma?"

"Oh beta, it's nothing. I had just been noticing..."

"That?"

"That you haven't been eating that well. So, I thought maybe you are bored of what I cook daily, and so, I decided to spice things up a little..."

"What again?"

"You just seemed to have lost your appetite, I mean... look, all you're nibbling onto is salad, even though there are such delicious desserts kept in front of you."

My forehead creased, "Listen, I know it's just that you care about me...but it seems like you're checking me Mumma, and lately, it seems like everyone has been checking me. The swimming coach, Ms. Yadav...the school doctor, dentist, *you*. And I just can't take it. So please, let me be."

"What happened at swimming and at the doctor?"

Oh shit. Why do I keep doing this? Why can't I keep my f*cking mouth shut?

My tone mellowed down a little as I explained myself, "Ms. Yadav said I have lost focus, and something of that sort..."

"But why would she say that beta?"

"Well, I really don't know. But the districts are on my head, and I really don't need any lecture from you as of now on one of the least important things on my mind – Food."

The Burning Truth

"Okay. Just...remember, we've got your back, and we're sure you'll do well."

I gave her a slight nod and smiled at her.

That night, I wasn't able to sleep quite well. I had so much on my plate. (Not literally, but figuratively). I couldn't stop thinking of how I was starting to look, I couldn't erase the image of those dingy, yellow hands. I couldn't help but agree, that I was hardly eating anything anymore, be it at home or at school. And most importantly, I kept thinking about how what I was doing (aka smoking) was affecting my swimming career, and I just couldn't think about losing districts, *I mean all this effort...for nothing?*

My brain had already worked overtime, and had been doing too much of thinking, so once again the lust of the temporary relief and joy took over me and I told myself, *I need to grab a smoke.*

The next morning, I woke up with a resolution.

No more smoking until districts, it was only distracting me and pulling me back, and I had no more time on my hands, districts were only a week away! That day, as I recall, I had even decided, that after districts, I'd eventually quit. I mean, who was I kidding, smoking won't do me any good...apart from *that wonderful, heavenly feeling I got every time I smoked a few cigs,* it was useless.

And with that, began the most lengthy, tiresome, and adventurous, week that I can never forget, even if I wish to.

52

4 DAYS LEFT

My districts were on Friday, the 30th of June. Which meant I had precisely only four days to polish up my game before the districts.

That morning, after one of the most tiring and lengthy early morning swimming practices, I went to apologize to Ms. Yadav for being a little distracted lately, and if I remember correctly, she said something on the lines of, "It's okay to get distracted once in a while, as long as you remember your way back. Now, stay focused, because the districts are in a week, and I want to see you at state level."

That was easy, I thought to myself. But what was coming my way next was the difficult part.

There were a few minutes left before the school started, so I headed to the steps, determined that I would not smoke. As I walked towards the steps, I could smell the smoke, travel up my nose, penetrating my body. As I stepped even closer, I could feel my mind pulling me towards the pack of cigarettes lying next to Natz, waiting for them to be opened and consumed. But I virtually slapped myself on the face and told myself, it's the wrong thing, and I've got to wait until districts, at least.

"Hey Sana, where were you?" Natz asked, seeming excited to see me.

"Well...that's what I wanted to talk about..." I replied hesitantly.

She took out the cigarette that was in her mouth, and let out the smoke that was stored. After a few seconds, she tapped out the ashes of her cigarette and she asked, "So, what is it?"

"Nothing much really...I just wanted to tell you that I have my districts... a swimming competition in about a week and so, I wouldn't be able to come for the morning session by the steps for a while. That's all... I guess."

Her eye twitched, and her nose flared, her posture suddenly became firmer. She took another puff and then questioned, "So, you are saying you can't come and sit with us in the morning...because of some competition you have that's coming up. Right?"

I knew I was dead. It felt like she was about to bombard me with questions and later kill me alive. I tried to maintain my calm and said, "Umm... Yeah."

"Okay Sana, no problem. You must focus on your competition, but don't you want to take one last smoke before?"

A loud, deafening bell rung in my head and a wrestling match between my mind and my brain commenced.

My mind was craving for another cigarette, for I hadn't smoked for almost 12 hours, and those twelve hours seemed way too long for me.

But on the other hand, my brain was screaming, don't smoke! It'll only pull you down, look your performance has already started to decline.

My mind hit my brain with even greater force, so what? Does happiness matter or some stupid competition?

My brain had a better comeback, think about your parents, your teacher, your dream. What happened to that? Do you not have even this much self-control?

My brain won that day. Thankfully.

"No Natz, I guess, I'm fine. But I'll see you guys after the competition, for sure...okay?"

"Alright darling, no worries at all. Do well!"

I couldn't believe it. She was so supportive, I thought she didn't hear me well or something of that sort. What I was expecting was her getting mad and angry for refusing a form of her friendship or some sort of privilege we got by hanging around with her. I was expecting for her to get angry for prioritizing my academic or rather athletic life over my social life, but she was so damn helpful and supportive.

That's the day when I knew, we were real friends. Because otherwise, she'd have probably reacted in some other cranky, snooty way, but instead she was supportive.

It was a miracle.

"So...you aren't angry?" I asked softly.

The corner of lips twisted upwards, "Why would I be?" she counter questioned me.

"Well...I thought you'd be not angry...maybe unhappy because you know, I'm refusing your invitation for the morning session...indirectly."

In a sing-along tone she replied, "Oh Sana...how naïve would that be of me? We are your friends...we care about you and your future. And I know this competition matters to you. So, of course we'll support you and not get angry because for some stupid reason." She said with utmost sincerity.

My lashes fluttered, trying to hold back the tears of joy that were about to fall from my eyes. I couldn't believe it. It felt like everything was falling back in place.

I smiled at her, and told her how much her saying this meant to me.

At my extra swimming lesson;

"Faster, faster, faster!!" screamed my additional swimming coach who taught me outside school.

He was a middle-aged man with a straight face and round eyes. His body was that of a perfect swimmer. He was a retired army instructor who now taught young 'aspiring' students like me. But he had *no clue* whatsoever about how to deal with students or children for that matter, and that was probably because of his army background. He often or rather always, scolded me even when I did things right, and that simply pissed me off.

I took out my head to breathe and saw him standing by the edge of the pool, with sweat dripping across his face and an unconditionally tensed and tired expression. I dipped my head back in and tried to swim even faster.

When I finally reached the end of the pool, I saw him coming towards me, with an expression I didn't want to see.

"What is the problem Sana?" He asked irritatingly.

"There's no problem sir. I am trying my best."

"No, you're not!" He shouted.

I closed my eyes and tried to calm myself down. I needed a cigarette, I was craving for a cigarette. But no, no smoking, I told myself.

"What are you waiting for? Five more laps. Freestyle. Go."

"Yes coach."

I took a deep breath in and started to swim towards the other end of the pool. I kicked as fast as I could, trying to fit in at least five to six kicks per rotation. I moved my hands just as I was told, in a way that I move aside the water. I maintained a perfect posture. But even then, when I finished my laps, the first thing he said was, "Try harder Sana! You are not going home until you beat your own timing, come on now!"

How can he just say that?

"Focus on you breathing. You are lacking there, taking too much time! Faster, c'mon!"

Should I not breathe now?

I moved my hands even faster, trying to cover up for the time I lost while I thought of ways to kill him. But it

The Burning Truth

didn't work. Because when I was done, he told me, "Your timing just got worse. What is happening Sana? Work harder. Now two final laps, try to spend less time on taking in air when you take your head out, and remember to go as fast as possible."

"Got it sir."

I put my head back into the water, and took a push from the wall, and my hands and legs started to move just the way they had been trained. Every time I had to take my head out for breathing, I'd try to take in air as quick as possible. When I got to the end, and finally took out my head to breathe, my entire body was groping for more air. It felt like my lungs couldn't handle the pressure of having to breath so fast. *It felt like they needed more time. I needed more time.*

I looked at my timing and I knew that I had improved by a few seconds, and I couldn't be happier. Finally, I saw some improvement.

"Sana...you need to work so much harder. The competition is less than a week away. I want better performance!" He said in an affirmative and taunting tone.

Are you kidding me? Can he ever appreciate me?

I bluntly thanked him, and walked towards home.

I remember feeling as if my brain was about to explode out of anger, and I wished that it would kill him along with me. I wanted to shout back at him and tell him, I am trying my best! How much faster can I go!? I realized that I should calm down and relax. I tried to take deep breaths, but they barely worked. I knew I needed a cig, for it felt like the pressure and the stress of districts in a week was killing me.

Thankfully, now I had a box of cigs almost everywhere. Be it my school bag, my lunch box, my swimming bag too for that matter. So, I took out a box of gold flakes. I looked at them for a while, contemplating my decision, I knew I had to be firm about not smoking, but it felt like I was under a magical spell of the cigs, whenever I thought of them, I couldn't resist them, and so, I ultimately gave up resisting at all.

I lit a cig and took some long puffs.

53

3 DAYS LEFT

'You should be ashamed of yourself. You couldn't even resist the craving for a few days? What happened to your decision? Did it get crumbled so easily? You should be ashamed of yourself...' The voice continued to echo in my head. *'You should be ashamed of yourself...ashamed...ashamed of yourself.'*

I woke up with a thud, the voice still ringing in my head. What had I done? I asked myself. Then, I recalled, lighting up a cig and smoking it last night, on my way back home, only because I was angry at the swimming instructor. I slapped myself in the face, a little too hard, and told myself sternly, 'You would not do that again.'

Then, I suddenly felt my phone buzz, so, I picked it up and opened WhatsApp. The first text, waiting to be read was from Natz. I quickly opened it and read it,

"Hey Sana, hoping your practice is going well...just wanted to check up on you, as a friend. I know that there are only three days to go...and I remember you telling us that three is your lucky number, so, I hope this day turns out to be lucky for you.

Love, Natz."

Aww. Although she sounded a lot like a boyfriend who was trying to be caring or something, it was so cute! She actually remembered, and she really did care. It was hard for me to believe that she was the same Natasha who tried to sabotage my entire life just because of some insecurities. But well, people change.

I hurriedly replied to her, because I didn't want to be late for morning practice, "That's so sweet of you to remember...I'm doing fine. Really missing you guys, gtg for practice now. Sys."

At morning swimming practice;

I could see the wall in front of me, just waiting there, waiting to be touched by one of the eight swimmers who were in the pool, including me.

"Move faster Dev! C'mon!" shouted Mr. Jain from the finishing line.

"Sana, you can do this! Focus, and just keep going. Move it! Faster! Faster! Faster!" shouted Ms. Yadav.

My arms executed alternating movements, and my legs were doing the flutter, six-beat kick. I inhaled quickly on the side of the recovering arm, and started to exhale as soon as the head rolled downward and continued to do so until the next breathing recovery.

But when I finally reached the end, I was still gasping for air.

"You made it to the top 5 Sana! Not bad."

"Really? I did?" I said as I beat myself on my chest, trying to fasten my air circulation, so that I can breathe better.

"Yes, yes you did." She told me with a smile on her face.

I nodded at her, because saying anything was simply tiring me out.

She continued, "You know, if you wouldn't have lost focus in between...and would've continued on the same track, I'm sure by now you'd be at par with Dev and all. But it's okay, we've still got two days left."

"Yes ma'am."

"Just do some breathing exercises, that's your weak point, make it your strength. Okay?"

At home, it was dinner time;

"How are the practices going?" asked Papa, who was seated next to Mumma, on the other side of the dining table.

"All good."

"That's all you have to say?" He asked with a mysterious expression.

"Okay...to further elaborate upon, the outside swimming coach is really strict. He gets angry for no reason, even when I'm doing everything I can."

"Hmm...But isn't that good?"

Good my foot.

"I mean, it's only going to help you improve, and that's what you need right now."

"Yes Papa."

No point arguing with him.

"Just remember one thing, do well and *win*."

Win! But that would only be possible if I'm able to breathe efficiently during swimming that time, it felt as though my entire body burned, my lungs ached, and my heart was on fire, every time I tried to breathe in air while swimming. Probably because I was a *young teenage smoker and it had somehow affected my lungs.*

Ewww. That sounded bad, even when I didn't speak it out aloud.

My thoughts were interrupted by Mumma, "Beta, we are really hoping that you'd do well...I mean, I'm sure you'll do well. But you can't even imagine the number of people we have to explain ourselves to."

Papa interrupted her in an aggravated tone, "You don't need to tell her all that Priya!"

"She deserves to know what you and I are going through because of her decision to swim Raj!"

"Okay. Go ahead, but don't over exaggerate. Please."

"See, I just want you to know...that people hear stuff. The entire family of mine and your dad's side are aware of you taking up swimming and have been quite curious about the whole thing. We've been telling them that you're going to ace this district event, and that you love swimming and all that, but they'll only be satisfied when they see that you've actually won or at least got something."

A line appeared between my brows, and my mouth twisted as I asked her, "Why are you telling me that Mumma?"

The Burning Truth

Papa replied instead, "Just so that you know...that there are a lot of people apart from us too, who are counting on you. That's all. Nothing else."

"Okay."

I picked up my plate and headed towards the kitchen, because I wasn't exactly sure of what I was expected to do.

As I walked back to my room, I heard Mumma and Papa whisper to each other in the background.

"Why did you have to tell her that?" asked Papa in a hushed tone.

"So that she knows that we're all really serious about this." She replied bluntly.

"Why can't you just let her be, you're simply pressurizing her."

And he was right.

I quickly escaped to my balcony, to grab a smoke. It was too much for me to handle. I took a long puff. And let it out from the nose. *How can they just go around telling everyone about the districts thing?* I took another puff and let it settle in my lungs, to get the kick. I exhaled again. *I mean, what if I don't win? What would happen then?* I took one more puff. *They have stressed me out so much. UGHHHH.*

They can't do this to me.

54

2 DAYS LEFT

"NOT AGAIN!!" I screamed in my mind.

Why do I keep doing this? What is wrong with me for God's sake? How do I manage to goof up every day for myself? Why can't I just for once stick by a goddamn decision?

I tried to console myself by thinking, that even though I did smoke yesterday and day before, it was much less compared to the number of cigs I was consuming when I used to sit with Natz's gang. So, that was a positive step, at least. I thought.

No time to waste, districts in a day.

❋ ❋ ❋

The morning swimming practice was fine, I was still somewhere among the top 3 people, same story different day. But something odd happened during our extra stay back after school for swimming which left me puzzled.

"Sana, today, for you, we only do breathing exercises. Okay?" Mr. Jain told me.

"Breathing exercises?"

"Yes Sana."

"But why?"

"Let me explain," Ms. Yadav butted in.

"Ahead you go." Said Mr. Jain.

"Look, we were observing each of our students carefully this morning, and we realized that you're doing everything right, the only place you are lacking is…breathing. Which is strange, since I recall when you joined the team, your breathing was perfect."

I replied with a confused expression, "Okay."

"So, today, you'll be practicing breathing. How to do it fast, swiftly and smoothly, such that you get enough air and don't start to suffocate or something. Got it?"

"Yes Ms. Yadav."

Thus, one day before my districts, all I did was see every other student practice their strokes vigorously while I simply revisited the concept of breathing properly, the credit for it goes to those dumb little cigs that were ruining my lungs, and probably my life even.

It was just so unfair, on the other side of the pool, Ms. Yadav was probably giving the other students expert tips on how to improvise, and how to win the competition, while I was stuck on this side, with Mr. Jain, *doing breathing exercises.*

What did I do to deserve this? Oh wait, I know, I illegally smoked and have now become addicted.

Makes sense.

When I reached home, I decided, no matter what happens, no matter what my mind says or craves for,

I would not smoke. I repeated "I would not smoke," throughout my bath, and even when I was lying in bed after dinner.

Then, my mind deviated for a little while when the bell rung, and once it stopped I was once again thinking about how Mumma and Papa have such high expectations, how if I don't win this time, they'd probably pull me out and tell me to focus on my academics, how this is literally my last chance. It all just got into my head.

And before I knew it, I had a cig stuck up between my lips, ready to be lit. With every puff I took, it felt like one of my questions faded away, and that's what I loved about this magical little rolled piece of paper, it held extraordinary powers to control one's mind.

55

A DAY LEFT

I HATE MYSELF.

Why do I keep doing this? It's districts tomorrow and because of this stupid habit I ended up doing breathing exercises yesterday instead of actual swimming. *Why can't I just stop screwing around and actually focus?* It's like these cigs have overpowered me in some way. They take over my brain, and just pull me towards themselves, and no matter how hard I try, I just can't stop.

But there is no other way, today *I would not smoke*. And I knew I'd see immediate results, at least that's what I hoped.

After the final morning regime;

My hands were all wrinkled and I could see some of my nerves popping out, my eyes had a thin layer of red blood clogged up towards the lower rim, my legs were shivering, not really supporting my body which now felt a little sore and numb.

Tired, exhausted, and half dead. That's how I felt right after our final morning regime before the districts.

That day, I saw all my teachers, even those who didn't really teach swimming, from a whole new perspective. Especially, Mr. Jain, who turned out to be surprisingly very inspiring and motivating. He constantly cheered for each one of us and kept saying things like "Push yourself" and "Harder" and "Faster."

I tried not to laugh, but is that really possible?

I didn't do that bad either, in fact, in my category, that day, I was able to reach the top two. I'd probably admit that it was because of bearing with that ex-army fellow, he was strict (and because of that I did end up smoking, *after quitting*) but he was also a great coach, and he just knew how to speed me up.

When we were doing our practice round, the only person who was ahead of me was The Wave, and that too, I missed him by a mere two seconds. Although, even now, when I came out of the pool, it felt like I could barely even breathe, while he seemed completely fresh as though he just came back from a swim at the beach.

That's when I figured, perhaps it's not because of the smoking that I'm having breathing issues. It's probably because I still have stamina issues, although I had improved a lot before I started to smoke, so I'm not sure. I don't even know what I'm saying anymore. My head was all cloudy again. There was a *khichadi* being cooked in my brain.

If I am not wrong, which I probably am not, that day, all swimmers were made to skip school and practice the entire day, which meant I was at the pool for exactly twelve hours, morning 6am to evening 6pm. Our practice session included the following:

- 10 rounds (minimum that is by the way) of the gigantic Olympic size soccer field.
- About 1 hour of random stretching and pulling and pushing and *God knows what.*
- Around 30 or maybe even more sprints.
- And the continuous, rigorous, torturous laps of the pool trying to perfect our stroke and improve our timing overnight.
- Out of those twelve hours, we precisely got 5 minutes of recovery time.
- Along with a 15-minute lunch break.

Now although these points given above seem highly exaggerated the points given above a little, but trust me, that is *exactly* how it was.

I was so exhausted that day that I ended up calling the driver right up to the swimming arena, because I no more had the willingness or the power for that matter, to pick up my swimming bag and carry it myself till the parking lot.

Another conflict was going on between my heart and my brain. On one hand, my heart was craving for a few cigs to relieve all the pain, while my brain, knew that these cigs would only cause more pain in the future. But for some odd reason, this time I was rooting for my heart, because I really did *need* a few puffs, otherwise it felt like my bones would crumble and fall apart into pieces. And I knew that just a few puffs could easily distract me from all the pain.

That night, I was too drained, and thus I didn't have the energy to escape to the balcony where Mumma and

Papa would not see me, and the smoke would get mixed with the air. So, I chose to simply smoke in my room, *it's not like they had cameras or something fixed in here*, I tried to convince myself. So, I opened my secret drawer in my cupboard which hid the stash and took out a cigarette to light it up in the room.

As I took long puffs, they miraculously seemed to wash away my pains, I opened my WhatsApp to find a text from Natz again. Before I could stop myself, my fingers quickly navigated such to open the message that said,

"Hey Sana, I know that you have districts tomorrow... see, I remembered! I wanted to wish you in person, but you were practicing the whole day... Anyway, we all just wanted to wish you the very best for tomorrow.

With love, Natz"

AWWWWW.

Best friends ever. Right?

56

THE DAY OF DISTRICTS: AT HOME

"Sana Sharma? *DID YOU SMOKE??*" shouted my Mumma at the top of her voice as she attempted to wake me up by shaking me vigorously.

Oh shit. I suddenly opened my eyes and it all came back to me, I recalled that I had smoked the night before, *in bed, in my room,* and forgot to spray the room freshener to kill the smell of smoke. I quickly turned my head around and realized that thankfully I didn't forget to extinguish the cigarettes which was good. Although I couldn't remember where I threw them exactly.

"Are you hearing me? Can you please respond Sana!?" She continued to scream.

Now, a good excuse could only save me. If there were no cigs around, then I could easily make up something, because the only proof that was there was the smell. *I could obviously make something up...But what?*

And that's when my eyes saw that the window was open. *Got it!*

"Enough is enough Sana Sharma! WERE YOU SMOKING OR NOT?" She shouted again.

"No Mumma, no!" I tried to reply in a calming tone.

"Then why does your room smell like smoke?" She continued to answer in a raised voice with her arms on her hips.

"Because of... our neighbors." I hesitantly lied.

Her face filled with anger, suddenly mellowed down and turned into a pale color. She blinked her eyes in a questioning manner as she asked, "What?"

"Well, I think their daughter...what's her name, Kareena...I think she smokes." I explained.

Great. Now I am openly lying to my Mumma. What is happening to me? Help me God.

"Oh my God, what a shame!" She exclaimed.

I nodded in agreement, "Now you see...she probably kept umm... her window open to let out the smoke...and someone probably left my door- no; window open."

"Hmm..." Mumma's face suddenly grew serious as she attempted to understand my broken theory behind the smoke.

"And then the smoke got into my room, see... that's why I have this room freshener kept here..." I said, pointing at it. "But the smell is just not going."

"Oh, okay beta...You should have come to our room, or the drawing room. One should always get a good night sleep before their big day...and today is yours." She replied, brushing her fingers through my hair, just as she did when I was a small girl.

I couldn't believe I had just lied to Mumma. I was suddenly hit by a wave of guilt. They cared so much about me, and I was simply lying, trying to cover up my tracks. She trusted me so much, that she agreed with whatever I said in a minute. How did I get here? What happened to me?

I plastered a smile on my face and told her that sleep didn't really matter. But I was wrong, because I was indeed feeling quite sleepy, and wanted to simply doze off, plus, I couldn't really recall how many cigs I smoked last night or when I went off to sleep.

"You should get ready now beta, and I'll get the breakfast ready."

"Okay Mumma."

✿ ✿ ✿

I was standing at the edge of the door, Mumma was standing opposite to me, and she had a golden plate, with some uncooked rice, red *tika*, and a *mithai*. Papa was there too, standing next to Mumma, and it turned out that he flew all the way from New York, just to wish me luck in person for my districts. He always goes to extremes. He either supports you, or he completely doesn't and until recently, it was the latter.

Mumma took some tika onto her ring finger, and applied it like a bindi, or a big red dot, right in the center of my forehead, in between my eyebrows. She then put some of the uncooked rice, or *Akshat*, onto that tika. And then at last, I was given some delicious rasgullas to savor on.

It was an Indian tradition that was followed every time one of the family members were about to embark on something new, go somewhere or do anything important, and Mumma would do this. I only liked it because of the mithais I got to eat in the end.

But for some reason, that day, all I could think about as I stood on the exit, waiting to leave for a big day ahead, was that *something was missing*. I was forgetting something, something really important. But what was I missing or perhaps forgetting?

I continued to think, but my chain of thoughts was disturbed when Papa suddenly started to speak, "Sana, I'm just glad that I am being able to give you something that I could not get…a chance. A chance to fulfill your dreams. A chance to live your life the way you want to. *Take this chance, and don't look back*. And remember, you are only going there to win."

I blinked my eyes slowly, telling him that I agree, and in a way thanking him at the same time.

Then, it had suddenly hit me, I needed a pack of cigs. That's what I was forgetting, that's what was missing! But no. Why would I need cigarettes? I would not smoke today, no matter what. It'll only pull me down. I told myself.

But the urge was strong, even though I wasn't smoking that instant, the thought of smoking had already taken over me, because my arms and legs were suddenly doing things I didn't want them to do. My arms quickly pushed apart Mumma and Papa, making space for my body to fit in and walked ahead through the gap.

My legs paced towards the room and right towards my hidden stash. I quickly took out my last two packs of gold flakes that were left and stuffed it in my swimming bag, as I did so, I said to myself, "Just in case. *Just in case.*" But deep down, I hoped that I would try and resist as well as avoid a situation where I would need to smoke a cigarette, for I knew it would only cause me harm.

"What happened beta?" asked Mumma, as I emerged from the door of my room.

"Oh um...I had, forgotten my sunglasses – no umm... swimming glasses. Yeah, that's what I forgot. Just went in to grab them. That's all Mumma." I told her.

She seemed perplexed, but decided to not interrogate further, "Okay beta."

"You should get going now Sana, it's getting late." Added Papa.

"Yes Papa, love you both. Bye." I said as I walked towards the bus stand.

"All the best!" They said in sync, shouting from behind me. "Win and come!" shouted Papa in an even louder tone.

I will win this time. I will win something. I will have to win.

57

THE DAY OF DISTRICTS: THE BEGINNING

We were all buzzing with excitement, and full of energy, well at least most of us. I was still a little drained out because of the less sleep from last night after all that smoking. All of us were seated in the audience area when I overheard the girls sitting behind me speak to each other.

"Have you heard of Samantha Brown?" asked a high-pitched voice.

The other girl replied in a hushed tone, "Isn't she the same girl who last year had a timing of..."

"37 seconds!" she completed her sentence.

"In 50-meter freestyle!"

"Everyone knows her."

I did not know her. And I did not intend to either since I feared that if she ended up against me, **I - Am - Dead.** My timing is absolute crap in front of her, if I am put to swim against her, forget gold, silver, or bronze, I'd probably be the last one to make it to the finish line.

The Burning Truth

Oh God. Too much stress.

"Mr. Jain is now coming to talk to the team," said Ms. Yadav.

However, some of my stress was released when Mr. Jain started to speak in his signature English, trying to motivate us. I tried not to laugh as he spoke, but it was inevitable!

"It's a *handsome* day today childs...today when we go to Modi Swimming center, we make history there. We win, and we enjoy. No matter what, I wish *two* medals, from each you. Now, go. And Win!!"

He then gestured Ms. Yadav to come and speak to us. She was back to being strict and stern, and no more of, 'you're my children' nonsense. She looked at us, and said, "There isn't much time to really do any prep-talking now. So, I'd just say one thing, put in your best. She paused and looked at me and continued, "And don't get distracted." *Why would she do that?*

"Let's just move towards the buses, alright? No time to lose! It's always better to be early than be late." She rushed us all out.

Typical Ms. Yadav.

In the bus, I decided to sit down and do some thinking while most of the other members of the team played a game called 'Who's that'? At that time, I thought, it's basically a game for nerds, not for *cool people like me who have super cool friends like Natz and Ansh.* In this game, kids got divided into two teams, and then, one team describes a famous swimmer's personality or character and the other team guesses the name.

As I closed my eyes, trying to immerse myself in deeper thoughts, various things came to my mind. A vague image of Mumma and Papa standing looking down, ~~on me~~, towards me came to my mind. I began thinking about Mumma and Papa, how much me winning in this competition meant to them. Gradually, my thoughts shifted to my own friends, my best friends. I could see them vaguely sitting on the steps, talking to each other, and all I could think about was how were all so supportive. Then I thought about Dev, I recalled him raising his hand, volunteering for becoming my buddy. And then at last, I thought about myself, how this was my dream, ever since I stepped foot in Avenues International, and how *all I wanted* was to win this damn thing and ultimately qualify for states.

When I opened my eyes, we had arrived at our destination: Kamla Modi Swimming Centre.

The waiting area was flooded with people varying from all age groups, to all classes. There were swimmers from all types of schools, including the top-notch private schools like Avenues International, Green Society as well as Shri Krishna.

Our team finally managed to find a little corner by the washroom, which was probably empty because it was stinking a lot. But no one really cared.

Ms. Yadav told us to make a tiny circle around her as she sat in between us, or rather in the center of us, with her arms crossed, and a serious face. She was about to give us her world-renowned prep talk, and I agree, I mean the last time she talked to me, I ended up convinced that

The Burning Truth

I must quit smoking, regardless of the fact that I failed later.

She took a deep breath and then started to speak.

"Today, you are here not because you were made for this, not because your parents told you to join, not because you aren't good at academics, and this is your only way out. You are here…because you *wanted* to be here. You *needed* to be–"

My phone suddenly started to sing, " La la la-la la la, Sing a happy song. La la la-la la la, your phone will ring all day long!"

Oh f*ck. Who could be texting me right now?

"I'm talking Sana. Can you please shut that down immediately!" She raised her voice at me.

"Yes Ma'am, I'm really sorry." I fumbled to find my phone and shut it down.

I quickly glanced over to see who's texted me, when I saw it was a text from Natz. *How sweet of her*, I thought. She must have texted to wish me best of luck before the races. I decided to take a look at it in a while, once Ms. Yadav was done speaking.

"Is it something very important Sana?" she asked sarcastically.

"No ma'am. Nothing important at all." I fidgeted with my phone, pushing it into my bag.

"Alright…So, as I was saying…You are here because… well I don't really remember what I was saying. So, let's just skip to the end. You are here to swim. And that's the end of the story." She paused for a second, and then she kind of shouted, "Now get up, and just...swim you guys!"

And even though her speech was broken and crooked, *thanks to my phone*...it was still oddly motivational and inspirational in its own funny way.

I was later told by Mr. Jain that my first event that was 50-meter freestyle was about two hours away. While my second event which was 100-meter freestyle was towards the end of the day. That meant, I had a lot of time to loafer around. Might as well make use of it.

I stepped outside the waiting room, and headed towards the adjoining park, it was comparatively quieter there, and I figured, I could use some peace before the competition. I found a quiet place to sit by which was under an orchid tree, the only people who were visible around were an old couple who seemed to be out on a date.

58

THE DAY OF DISTRICTS: CONFESSION #1

The first thing I chose to do was open the text that was waiting in my WhatsApp unread messages. I was correct indeed, the first message was from Natz, *how nice of her*, I reiterated in my mind.

But that was not exactly how I felt when my eyes actually read the message which changed my life.

Hey Sana,
How are you feeling? All prepared? Who am I kidding again? I don't really care…

Why would she say that? I knew she cared. But for a second it felt like she was taunting me the way she did when we were enemies. But then I tried to console myself by thinking, *she must be joking... of course she cares!*

It continued to read;

So, my sources tell me, you are yet to enter the pool for another few hours at least. And well, being the good friend that I am…

HOW DOES SHE KNOW THAT? Was this all some sort of a *joke?* It had to be one, I mean we are best friends, I literally changed my entire personality for her, and started to smoke because of her...and started to lie because of her. Okay, I'm going off topic, let's read ahead. It said; being the good friend that I am...I decided to give you some things to ponder upon before the competition, to make sure you don't get bored.

> So, here's my first confession, remember your first, close/only friend at Avenues International – Ansh Roy – the guy from your bus? The guy who invited you to the party? The guy who introduced you to smoking?

Of course, I remembered him. He was the only guy who I talked to initially, before I got close to Dev. He was the guy who I basically trusted my life enough with that I let him make me do something which I wouldn't ever do in my normal senses – make me smoke. The message continued;

> I hope you didn't wind up thinking that he just liked you for your wit and charm and all that nonsense. In case you did, let me get this clear for you: I told him to become your friend. I told him to invite you to the party. I told him to introduce you to smoking, and in case you're wondering why I did this, I'll let you know in my next confessions to come.

*What the f*ck was she talking about?*

It felt like I wasn't in control over my body anymore, because at that moment, all I wanted to really do was simply go and punch Ansh and kick his balls. I would have seen him cry with pain and only then would have let him go.

My brain started to work like a machine, fueled with sudden-found hatred towards him. How in the bloody world could he do this to me? I trusted him. I befriended him in an unknown territory and this is what he did to me? Betray me? Lie to me? *That bastard.* But instead of punching him and beating him down, I chewed on a cuticle and continued to read;

> I hope this gives you something to think about. Now, why don't you go and smoke a few cigs to calm down?
> With love,
> Natz
> (Your bestesttt friend)
>
> Ps. Once you are done scratching your head about this one, just remember there are four more confessions still left.

Tears filled my eyes, as I scratched my head, trying to figure out what to do. *Stop scratching your head!* I screamed internally. That's exactly what she wanted me to do!

A million thoughts clouded my head.

I sat, with my butt against the cold rods of the bench, with my legs crossed, and my head buried in my folded hands, trying to hide away the waterfall that was flowing through my red eyes. I wasn't really sure anymore as to how I was feeling, whether I was simply depressed because of her, or if I was angry at her. All I was certain about was that I *needed* a cigarette to calm myself.

Thankfully I carried my box of gold flakes, for a 'just in case' situation, I didn't have the time to think about the consequences or after effects, all I cared about was calming myself down and not acting out in front of everyone, so, I quickly shoved my hand inside the swimming bag, to find a box of cigs, and within no time, it was placed between my index and middle finger, ready to relax me.

As I took some long puffs, I noticed that the old couple was staring at me, but to be honest, I hardly cared. With the first pull, I started to think about Ansh. It felt like I had been *punched in the gut.* As I shut my eyes, trying to digest everything, a blurry image of him and I talking on my first day in the bus, and then one when I asked him where my classroom is, appeared in front of my eyes. Then, another rather vivid image of him and I helplessly banging into each other at the staircase popped up into my head. I remembered sitting next to him, with my head on his shoulder and tears suddenly filled my eyes.

We had built so many memories, *were they all based on lies?* I asked myself as I carried the smoke into my lungs and out through my nose.

Next, I started contemplating about Natz. I kept asking myself again and again was, *why would she do that?* Was it all a part of some sort of plan to distract me by her texts *right before* my competition? No, that can't be true! She wouldn't do that...she *is* was my best friend.

As I smoked my second cigarette, finally a relaxing thought came to my clouded and very troubled brain and I knew the nicotine was doing its job. I started to think, what if she is *not* being a rude ass bitch who tried to play with my mind and soul for almost a month, but instead she was simply trying to be true and honest with me? Maybe she simply didn't really want to build our friendship on *hate and lies*, and that's why she was trying to tell me the truth...

The edges of my mouth twirled up a little as I finally had the chance to think of something positive. When I finally lifted my head, out of my arms cocoon, I suddenly felt like a pair of eyes, that did not belong to the old couple were looking at me from a distance, watching my every move.

A chill ran down my spine, and the wind suddenly grew cold.

59

THE DAY OF DISTRICTS: CONFESSION #2

I saw the eyes, staring at me and then hiding behind the semi-circular block structure that was the entrance to the park, which connected the swimming pool to the area I was sitting in. *Who was watching me?* I wondered.

I glanced at my watch, and realized that there were still about forty-five minutes left for my heat to begin, so I had time to send Natz a quick reply and then go check and see who was snooping around me. So, I picked up my phone to reply and tell *her how wonderful it was of her to choose to tell me the truth about her past instead of building our relation on lies,* when my phone started to ring again "La la la-la la la, Sing a happy song. La la la-la la la, your phone will ring all day long!"

I thought, it must be Mumma, texting me to wish me all the best, but instead, it was another message from Natz. I figured, she must have texted me to apologize about having to tell me the truth at such a crucial point,

The Burning Truth

causing me to smoke about two cigarettes right before my districts. I swiftly opened the text which told me;

Hi Sana,

Feeling a little better? Did those cigs help you calm down from the trauma you just faced? Well, I hope so…or do I?

How in the world did she know that I was smoking? Now, I was sure someone was spying on me. In that completely empty park (the old couple had already left) I knew I wasn't quite alone, for there were definitely a pair of eyes that were looking over me, and it was not in a good way.

The text continued;

Nevertheless, keep a few more cigs handy since I have my second, and rather bigger confession to make. You'd really like this one.

Remember the party where you first smoked? Well, it was all organized and planned by me. And do you recall how exactly did we become friends? I guess you'll say no. And that's because we never exactly became friends. That night, you were so high after three cigarettes itself, that when you came to me… we dumped you in a corner and went away, and then made up the whole story of how we became friends afterwards…

Now it made sense why I couldn't recall how I ended up in that dirty, disgusting corner when Mumma had asked me. In fact, it all made sense now; be it about how we became friends, or how we came so close within a matter of one night.

That cigarette was no *VIP access*! It was just a bloody way of making a fool out of me. That was also probably the reason why when I tried to ask Ansh how I ended up in such a position, he neglected me, and instead I ended up smoking even more.

Everything seemed so crystal clear. Everything *except* why was Natz doing this?

The message finally ended with this;

> I guess…you now have a lot to think about, I'll text you in five minutes…until then, why don't you smoke a cigarette or two?
> Love,
> Natz
>
> (Your best friend…who am I kidding?)

Oh God. Why was this happening?

I closed my eyes shut, as tight as possible, and tried to hold back the tears. There was no point crying! I told myself. So, what, if one of my first, and only best friend turned out to be playing against me? So, what, if I felt broken, cheated, betrayed and dismayed on the inside? It didn't matter, did it?

Out came another cigarette, the only thing that was there for me, when everyone bailed out. The only thing that would stand by me, no matter what. The only thing I could really trust to make me feel happy again, the only thing I had control over...*or was it the thing that controlled me?*

By then, my thoughts were all jumbled and my brain was barely making any sense, there was simply too much going on in my head. I took a long puff, trying to take the smoke as deep as possible to get a greater kick, to forget everything that had happened in the past few minutes and everything that had been happening with me for the last few days.

But that day, until then, all I kept wanting to ask her was, *why was she doing this?*

60

THE DAY OF DISTRICTS: HEAT 1

"We have been trying to find you everywhere! Why are you here?" Asked The Wave.

I tried to wipe away my tears as fast as possible, for I didn't want any questions being asked. My voice was shaky and my eyes were swollen, but I finally replied, "Umm...I'm sorry, did I miss something, what's happening?"

He placed his hands on his hips, and stepped a little closer to the bench I was sitting on, "Wait, were you crying or something? What is this about...first time swimming? That's why?"

Thank God, now I could use that excuse! I mean, it's better than, going around telling everyone that my best friend actually controlled and kind of ruled over the very few friends I ever made at Avenues, and chose to tell me all this right before the districts for some odd reason which I fail to understand.

I replied with a little hesitation, "Yep, just...a little...scared."

He smirked, and said under his breath, "New comers..."

My mouth was willing to tell him the truth, but I tried to smile instead, "Yes...newcomer!"

"Alright, now come on, we've got to go, you're up in few minutes."

Oh God! I let out a big sigh, and said, "Okay, yep. I'd be there in a sec."

Somehow, I managed to get so distracted that I completely forgot about why I came here, my districts! I checked my watch that told me I had only about eight minutes before my race began. *I'm screwed.*

After smoking four cigarettes, one after the other, I had obviously some issues in thinking straight. My head felt a little heavy, while I could feel something was building up in my stomach. I realized that 'The Wave' was still waiting for me to follow his lead, so I had no option but to simply stay shut and go with him.

"You need to change, hurry!" The wave continued.

My words were slopping a little, as I tried to speak, "Yeah, I'll umm...do that. Just give me a min...ute."

I grabbed my bag and headed to the changing room, where I faced a new challenge. Every time I bent my head down, in order to locate where my legs need to go in the swimming suit, I felt nauseous and sick. I tried to slap myself in the face, so that I was able to stand straight, but even when I did that, it seemed as if I was standing still but the world was spinning around. It felt like I was jerry and every time I tried to get into my bill, it just magically kept moving on the wall.

"Can't you just stay still? I am trying to do something here!" I yelled at the whole that was made for the leg in my swim suit.

After a few minutes of discomfort and acrobatics, I finally managed to fit myself in the swim suit. As I paced outside the cubicle, I changed my path and went to the basin instead. I looked at myself in the pale, rusty mirror, with cracked and broken edges, just like me. But the person who I saw, was definitely not Sana Sharma.

It was rather a young girl, who on the outside, had red, swollen eyes, and teeth which were pale, her hands now seemed a mustard color, and lips which were turning black. But her condition from within was worse, for all she was struggling to understand was the answer to one simple question, *how did she get here?*

"Sana, it's your heat in a minute, we need you up here."

I didn't look back, but I knew it was Ms. Yadav who was peeking through the door and calling out for me, hoping that I'd do something, get something, win something. But now I had begun to question if that was really going to happen.

I vigorously splashed some water onto my face, in an attempt to look a little normal and alive, instead of dead and done. Then patted my face using both my palms one after the other, trying to pull myself out of the imaginary world created by the nicotine in the cigarettes.

"Sana Sharma, Lane 6" announced a shrilly voice on the microphone.

Oh damn, it's my turn.

My hands and legs worked simultaneously as my arms threw away my swimming bag onto the exit of the changing room, while my legs tried to run as fast as they could, straight towards my block which was right at the end of the pool since I was in the last lane.

As I stepped onto the block, I fantasized stepping onto this magical podium that had the power to transport me to another world. For that brief minute between the emcee calling out my name, and the starter starting the heat, multiple thoughts raced through my mind.

I looked around myself, and to my right were a set of five swimmers, who seemed fitter than ever, they had slim, streamlined bodies and swimmer legs. Two of them were stretching, but then it hit me, due to all the texts and smoking, I forgot to stretch! So, I decided to simply replicate what the swimmer to my right was doing, because it seemed like I had completely forgotten about my entire swimming regimen.

As I did a 180 degrees twist, to stretch out my arms, I saw that my swimming team was cheering for me, rather screaming, "You can do this Sana!" and that's when I saw Dev, his face seemed a little off, as though he wasn't sure about what's going on. I had expected him to cheer for me, after all, he was my support system in the swimming team, but for some reason, he just stood there, not saying a word. But I didn't have much time to analyze what was happening, because suddenly, the referee said, "On your mark!"

I took a long breath, and was ready to dive, kneeling down, holding onto the block. It felt like I didn't even know what I was doing, it all just came to me, naturally, like a rehearsed dance routine. And before I knew it, the loud horn blew.

For the next few seconds, my brain completely stopped functioning, all I could think about was that finishing line. I darted towards it with my legs and hands moving in coordination and simultaneously. My hands rotated like a Ferris wheel, one following the other. My legs were beating the water with all force as I performed a six-beat kick, and everything as told by Ms. Yadav. But *I needed more air.*

I soon knew that my lungs were giving up on me, my body needed more air. But I couldn't stop, I told myself. I looked to my right, which obviously decreased my speed, and saw that among the six of us, I was the second-last. *Shit.*

Come on Sana, you can do this, I tried to motivate myself. *Faster, faster and faster.* I kept repeating. But it seemed to me that my body wasn't really listening to what my mind was saying. Even then, I kept going. I just couldn't give up, and plus I knew I was more than halfway through.

"Go Sana! Go Sana! East or west, Sana is the best!" My swimming team was shouting. God no, I wasn't the best, *couldn't they see I was losing this thing so badly?* I finally took out my head and took one long breath, and then jolted forward, with as much force as I could put in, pushing, rather tearing through the water. That's when I realized, short breaths won't work for me, my body needed more air, *I needed more air.*

I could see the wall waiting to be touched, right ahead of me, and I could also see the froth trail left behind by the three other swimmers, in front of me. If not first, I still could win a bronze if I am able to overtake one more swimmer. I focused all my energy into my arms, for I knew they were my strength, I took one last, long breath, and paced forward.

My hands were moving rapidly in anti-clockwise rotation, chasing one another, but not really catching one another, regardless of their speed. My feet were flipping up and down, just like we were taught, with our legs completely straight, as fast as I could. I stopped thinking about which skills are to be applied or what I was even doing. All I knew was that I was swimming to win that damn race.

I may have been about 10 meters away from the finishing line, when I suddenly heard a big group of swimmers screaming and shouting, followed by the referee's first whistle. This meant that the first position, i.e. the gold medal was gone. *So, what?* I still had the second and third position to fight for. I tried to put in even more power, but it felt like I was in an endless desert, trying to reach the oasis which seemed to only go further away from me.

Another swimming team suddenly screamed "You did it! Way to go Geetika!" followed by the second whistle from the referee, now this simply meant, the four other girls in the pool, including me, were fighting for one position. The entire stadium suddenly fell silent, and the only sound that I could hear was of our legs flipping up and down.

I swiftly yet slowly turned my head to an angle of about 90 degrees, such that I was able to see that another swimmer was literally a millimeter away from me. And in that friction of second when I turned my head around, and she glanced back at me, she crossed me, covering the one millimeter, and before I knew it, the last and final whistle blew.

Oh my God. I had definitely not come first, or second, or third, or fourth or anything. What I achieved was the *last position.*

I had lost.

❁ ❁ ❁

"You can't always win, but you can always try." Ms. Yadav tried to console me by patting me on the back gently.

"Yes ma'am." I told her, as I fixated a fake smile onto my face.

"It is okay Sana, you still is to swim your 100-meter race, you go and win that. Right?" Mr. Jain asked me, in an attempt to motivate me.

"Yes sir." I replied.

About ten minutes later, I was *still* panting for air, it felt like that one race had soaked up every single molecule of oxygen that was present in my body. I needed some air, figuratively and literally. So, I put on a towel and grabbed my swimming bag, and started to walk back towards the bench where I was sitting earlier inside the park which was adjoining the swimming arena.

I kept my head lowered down, so that no one recognized me, because I was the one who was beaten by another swimmer by a fraction of a second, just because of my idiotic mistake of looking back. But even then, I could feel eyes glaring at me, I could tell that people were talking about me, and *it did not feel nice*. So, I then took the towel, wrapped myself, covering my head as well and then began to walk towards the park.

61

THE POST-BREAK UP — BREAK UP

I started to rush ahead, trying to get away from everyone when I suddenly banged into Ria. *Yes, Ria* my best friend from Florens Public School. It was the same Ria.

She was dressed in her cheerleader's costume, a typical short skirt, a top which was way above the 'tank top' zone coupled with sneakers and a high ponytail. And although she still appeared no better than me, it seemed like Aman (*yes, Aman*) and his friends were still swooning around her.

While on the other hand, my hair was a mess, because I had just taken off my swimming cap, my eyes were still red, I was wearing a towel like a *ghoongat*, I had just lost a race because of something *really stupid*, and was about to go and smoke another cigarette to calm the shit down. I was disgusted on how the tables turned, and was unable to hold myself together.

As I thought about all this and evaluated the situation, she continued to stare at my blank face as though I was some person who was in desperate need of a lot of pity and a smiley face.

And that is exactly what she gave me. It seemed like one of those post-breakup meetings when one of the two's life sucks and the other is acing it, and even trying to rub it off in the sucked one's life. The sad part was, I was the one with the f*cked up, crumbling life, while she was the one who had seemingly won the break up.

"Hey...Sana, how are you doing?"

Are you kidding me? That's what you choose to ask me after not replying to my calls and messages for like ages? That's what you should say after betraying me, taking over my empire and literally cutting me off from your entire life? This day could not get any worse, or at least that's what I thought.

"I'm doing just fine. What about you, Ria?" I said while raising an eyebrow in question.

"Well, I'm fine too..." She replied hesitantly.

Wow, I couldn't believe she was the same person with whom I had shared my deepest darkest secrets, had midnight conversations with, and fought the world with. It was all so different.

My eyes widened, and my eyebrows knitted as I asked, "So...you're here, for?"

"Cheering for my...friends." She replied with a big-fake-smile on her face.

Friends who were at some point fan followers of mine, who once had created an IG page, just because they worshiped me. Yep, the same friends. *And what about me? Who am I to her now?* A past acquaintance, is that what she would tell her 'friends' when they ask about me?

"Right." I replied bluntly.

A moment of awkward silence followed.

"You swum...well." She said with a pitiful face.

Well? Wow, how generous of her to say that. I pressed my lips together, and through gritted teeth said thanks.

My phone suddenly started to buzz, "La la la-la la la, Sing a happy song. La la la-la la la, your phone will ring all day long!" OH God, IT'S NOT A GOD DAMN HAPPY DAY. SHUT THE HELL UP, is what I wanted to say, but it actually rescued me from the awkwardest situation.

I quickly glanced at my phone and informed, "I think it's my mom." It was a text, and it was *not* from my mom. It was another text from Natz. But I obviously wouldn't tell my ex best friend about my other best friend who recently became my ex best friend and revealed how my entire life at Avenues was basically a lie (I know it's complicated).

She nodded as though I had said something extremely important, "Sure, you must take it."

"Yeah, I'll...I'll see you around." I said, as one corner of mouth twisted upwards.

"Sure... bye." She replied with squinted eyes, as though she was in a rush to just, go, *get away from me*.

I clearly remember even today, that as I began to walk away, towards the park, just waiting to get away from everybody's eyes, to grab a smoke, Ria called out for me again from the back and I just stopped there. In slow-motion, I turned around, without saying anything.

"Aman is here too." She shouted.

And the day just got a little more worse.

"In case you wanted to meet him..." she murmured under her breath.

Sure. Why wouldn't I want to meet him? The same guy who first made me dream about him, made me feel that we were the perfect duo and then made me believe that he 'loved' me, followed by him *crushing my enormous heart with so much love in it, into tiny, small, grain-sized pieces.*

My mouth twitched a little as I told her, "You know what, there is some unfinished business, I might as well take this opportunity and meet him."

She seemed a little taken aback, as though she wasn't expecting that I'd agree to her offer, but she responded, "Yeah...sure."

I followed her as she walked towards the stall where the FPS swimmers were seated. With each step I took, I thought about everything he had done so far, to first lead me on, and then hurt me and tear apart my precious soul.

And maybe it wasn't just him I was angry at, maybe it was the kick from the three-four cigarettes, coupled with how angry I genuinely was with my life, that as soon as I saw him, I kicked him hard! Slapped his face left and right. Clenched my fists and punched him. Screamed, "You are a f*cking jerk!" and ran away.

That felt nice.

62

THE DAY OF THE DISTRICTS: CONFESSION #3

This day just can't get any worse. I told myself, as I took out my phone from the swimming bag that hung on my shoulder. I contemplated about all that had happened that day.

The following set of things had happened in the past 180 minutes:

1. I lost a race which I had been preparing for over two months because I was kind of high. I was feeling like puking all the time when I sawm. My arms and legs were paining because of not stretching properly. My lungs were craving air and my brain was stupid enough to look back and loose.

2. I found out that my first best friend (*Ansh*) at Avenues International was not really my best friend but was told by my kind of ex-best friend (*Natasha*) to be my fake friend and make me smoke in the first place.

3. My actual best friend (*Ria*) turned out to be a bitch, who never replied to all the texts I sent, and then randomly

The Burning Truth

saw me *lose* in a competition which meant so much to me, and then made fun of me with her friends.

4. A party for which I fought with my father, turned into a rebel, and broke all rules, turned out to be a party which was simply a manipulative move for introducing me to smoking in the first place.

5. And worst of all, I go and kick my ex in his nuts and tell him that he's jerk in front of everyone who'd now make fun of me for the rest of my life even if I don't really meet them again.

Yep. *This day can't get any worse.*

I finally opened the text, hoping she would apologize for everything she did, or that she was just being stupid, and now regretted it. Or maybe just say sorry. But then, I guess that's the problem with me, *I always try to find the best in the worst people.*

Here's what the text told me;

Hey Sana,

So, I heard you couldn't win the last race…

HOW IN THE BLOODY WORLD DID SHE KNOW THAT???

I am actually surprised you even went for it, considering that I gave you so much to think about. Well, it seems that that wasn't enough, so, here's my third confession.

Remember how I invited you to join me for the morning session by the steps? I'm sure you remember. It's not a thing one forgets easily…

Duh, I mean, I thought it was an honor when she invited me to come and join them…I didn't sleep that night out of happiness and joy. Just for the sake of attending those sessions, I fought with my coach, Ms. Yadav and to some extent, even disrespected her, putting my future swimming career in danger.

"Well, those morning sessions were actually just staged by my gang and I so that we can get you hooked onto smoking, and while we smoked ecstasy…which is actually nicotine-free, you smoked more and more nicotine and tar, every day, and got addicted. Funny you never noticed.

Ps. Don't throw away your phone just yet, because in my next confession I would finally answer to your question: Why the hell am I doing all this?"

Stay tuned,

Natz

Great. My day just got so much better!

I stuck up the fifth cigarette of the day in my mouth and started to smoke, and the first thing that came to my mind was: *What am I doing?* It didn't take me much long to understand, that I was obviously addicted. Addicted to the feeling of constantly feeling nice, even when nothing good was happening. Hooked onto the habit of curing all my troubles using a 7 cm long miraculous sheet of paper which contained the treasures of the world, and I would blame Natz for all this, but it was also me. After all, it was I who chose to become friends with her in the first place.

Why else would I be taking something that has caused so much destruction and devastation in my life?

I started thinking about how I managed to be so blindsided towards them such that I never realized what

The Burning Truth

I was getting into. I then began wondering whether it was me being blindsided or me simply trying to surpass the harsh reality of what I was getting into. As I took another pull of my cigarette, flashes of all of us sitting on the steps – *laughing, enjoying and smoking* came to my mind. I saw a nostalgic glimpse of Ansh laughing with his nose flaring, like it always did when he laughed. Then a flashback of Ria, Aman and I at our movie outing came to my head, I suddenly felt goosebumps thinking about them, and the hair at the back of my neck stood in place.

My body shrunk in size, and tears welled up in my eyes. I tried to hug myself by wrapping around my one hand that was still empty, but the cold breeze coming from the tree under which I still sat, seemed to make me feel cold.

I kept asking myself again and again, *what is wrong with me?* But another question overpowered this one when I started to think, *why was she in fact doing all this?*

63

THE DAY OF DISTRICTS: CONFESSION #4

I squinted my eyes to look at my watch, trying to read the time but this time, instead of bending my head downwards, I chose to raise my phone to read the time, otherwise I knew I'd puke all over myself and probably the bench – which was now my only hiding spot, right in the center of a mysteriously dark and empty park.

Based on my calculations I had about three hours before my final race, i.e. 100-meter freestyle and I knew to win this race, I had to pull myself up, forget about everything that had happened in the past few hours and most importantly, *not smoke* because I knew that if I smoked one more cigarette, it would break my record of number of cigarettes in a day and it would mean I had consumed...much *more than 60 grams of nicotine*, and considering my current state of mind, and more importantly heart, it would be *too much for me*.

Hence, I made a firm decision, I would get rid of the cigarettes that I was left with in order to avoid any future usage. I knew that was the best decision at that time. So, my eyes quickly scanned the area, figured that a place away from the swimming arena would be a safe place to throw them to, since the park was basically isolated.

So, I kept my swimming bag aside on the bench, took out my box of cigs, held it tightly in my hand and started to walk towards a bush that was about 20 meters away from me. I tried to sing a song, trying to distract myself from the thought of smoking, considering that there were so many things going on in my mind which needed to be cooled off, and a smoke could *really help* me right now.

"Hmm hmm, hmm...happy clap along...if you feel like...hmm hmm hmm, is the truth..." I tried to sing, but really who was I kidding, how can I sing about being happy when *the only truth* was that it was by far *the worst day of my life.*

All I could possibly hope now for was that I'd not smoke a single more cigarette, and do my best for the 100 meters by utilizing the time I had for stretching, exercising, practicing my strokes, and most importantly, sobering up.

Yes, that's exactly, *precisely, accurately, undoubtedly*, what I thought of doing.

"La la la-la la la, sing a happy Song. La la la-la la la, your phone will ring all day long!" For God's sake! How does this phone with artificial intelligence and all that crap not understand, it's not a happy day and I am not going to sing a fricking happy song!

I knew it was a text from Natz, *who else could be texting me right now?* And even though I knew I shouldn't look at it, I was tempted to look at it one last time. I tried to fight with my brain that was stopping me from looking at it.

Hence, I ultimately ended up giving into the desire to see what the message said, and I regret it even today.

I held the box of cigarettes, ready to be disposed in my left hand, and my phone with a message from Natasha in the other hand. I did think of throwing the pack of gold flakes away first but *God knows what* took over me, that I decided to read the message before throwing the pack of cigarettes away. And that is what caused all the problems that followed.

This is what I read;

Hey Sana,

I am actually getting kind of bored of this lame little game of ours. Although I am sure it is keeping you occupied, leaving you with lots of things to think about and question every life decision you've made till now. (See, I can be funny too!)

Seriously? If there was a thing like punching through the phone, I would've surely done that, but I sadly couldn't. So, I just stood there, completely still, with my slouched back, and my eyes fixated on the screen. And yes, I was already questioning my entire existence. Oh God. *I made zero sense.*

Anyway, coming back to the point, here is my final confession: Dev, your so-called buddy, or best-friend, or whatever you think of him to be in your dreams, well I had told him to keep a track on you as well, so that he can update me about each move of yours. He was nothing but

The Burning Truth

> a spy. After all, why else would he just randomly choose to get so close to you? I hope you didn't think it's because you have common classes and common interests like…
> swimming.
>
> Keep thinking, and smoke a cigarette, it'll only help you. Trust me.
>
> Your well-wisher,
> Natz.

I suddenly lost grip of the box of cigarettes that was in my other hand which fell on the grass next to my feet. *I couldn't take it anymore.* My head felt too heavy for my body to take its burden, and before I knew it, I collapsed on the ground and stayed there for the next few minutes.

It felt like I had blacked out, but could still hear and feel everything. I could feel the fire of anger and betrayal that was heating the insides of me. I could feel the punch in my gut, I could feel the sting in my heart.

I could feel it all, and yet I felt so numb.

64

THE DAY OF DISTRICTS: FINAL VERDICT

Time doesn't stop, this isn't a magical fairytale or a Bollywood film after all. Time keeps running, and no matter what, it would not stop. It didn't stop for me, and it probably won't stop for you either, *unless, you're Shah Rukh Khan, of course.*

And so, I simply lay there, on the emerald colored grass, with ants crawling by next to me, and a ladybug flapping its tiny little red wings with polka dots in front of my eyes. The box of gold flakes was in my reach, and so was my phone. But for that moment at least, it felt like I had a brain and body freeze.

A few minutes later, I finally decided to pull myself up. For I knew, that in reality there are no prince Charmings, dressed in Godly attires that would come and rescue a girl who is high and depressed and clueless about what she's doing in life because of her *psychopath, ex-best friend.*

Regardless of how *shocked, betrayed, tortured and hurt* I was, I was still determined to throw away my cigarettes, because at that time the only goal I was trying to focus on, was winning the 100-meter heat, and shoving it into Natasha's stupid little face.

So, I grabbed the box and was about to chuck into the bushes, when my phone started to ring again, "La la la-la la la, Sing a happy song. La la la-la la la, your phone will ring all day long!" What the hell? It felt like even my phone was taunting me and being sarcastic about how sucked up my life was.

It suddenly clicked my mind, the message was probably Natz's final confession about *why the hell was she creating all this drama.*

I thought, I've faced so much trauma, *what would one last text do*? And so, I decided to open it, and this is what I read on the screen,

Sana,

Now, I know all this while, all you've been wondering about is *why did I do all this*? And so, I thought, what's the point in tormenting your already tampered brain and heart? So, here it goes as to why I chose to make you first start smoking and then get you addicted to it:

Dev.

Yes, him. The guy who you supposedly had started to really like, trust and what-not. Well, he is the same guy who motivated me to pull you down by distracting your tiny-little, desperate-for-attention mind.

It was simple, he wanted to win the districts, and qualify for the states, and from the very beginning he knew that you were his only competition. So, it was in common interest of the both of us to bring you down, and hence, I put along this entire plan: the party, the morning sessions, and these texts.

Oh, and I almost forgot to mention the other reason of me doing all this -

The war.

I hope *you* didn't forget about it. Remember I told you, "the war is on"? Well I meant it, and today, it will finally come to an end, because I would at last accomplish what I had always wanted - to see you lose, and that's exactly what will happen today. Twice. And when you lose today in front of not only your swimming team and teachers, but also your friends from the last school, you would regret ever choosing to begin a war *against me* in the first place.

Because today is the day when -

I win, and you lose.

I've been waiting for this day since so long, and now that it's here, all I am left to say is, you go and rot in hell and die, you f*cking bitch.

Natz.

My jaw went slack, and my lower lip trembled. I was blanched, my eyes drooped and my face was washed with sudden pain and sorrow.

The words "I win, and you lose" resonated in my ears, and my hands suddenly began to shiver. I shook my head in disbelief, she was not Natz, or Natasha, she was rather Natzi, for he was the only person who believed that killing innocent people for his own sake was acceptable. And isn't that exactly what she was doing? Taking away an innocent, simple and harmless child's life, and flushing it down the toilet.

I was suddenly overwhelmed with all my feelings, all my emotions, everything that I should have had been feeling but the cigarette was stopping me from feeling was now coming to me, all at once. I suddenly felt hopeless and dumped while I had begun to believe lately that I was part of the most sought-after group in school. This didn't seem or feel good. I wanted an end to this self-acquired agony, *the pain, the shock, the hate, the disgust.* And worst of all, the feeling of simply wanting to give up on hope - hope that tomorrow will be a better day.

The surge of thought kept sprouting and making my heart as well as my soul darker with every passing second. I didn't even know why, but I simply picked up my phone, tightly clenched it in my fists, and then threw it as far as I could. It was not long before I realized that I could no more reply to her texts or read anything further.

A nauseating feeling began to take over me.

Why did I do this?

After getting rid of my phone, I committed a crime for which I am solely to be blamed for I smoked another three cigarettes. When my mind was still not satisfied, I took out the content of the next two cigs and consumed it directly. 10 cigarettes = one day.

Worst mistake ever.

65

THE LAST TURNING POINT
THE DAY OF DISTRICTS: HEAT 2

"Are you sure you want to do this?" Ms. Yadav asked me with eyes filled with concern, and a face that couldn't be any more tense.

"Yes... Yes. I'm sure. I want to."

"You have obviously smoked, I am sure of it since you have a terribly bad breath, and you're coughing continuously. Plus, you don't really seem that well." She said, as she examined my face.

"Trust me, I'm fine. I need to...do this thing, and just prove to some people, and myself, that I have some worth. Even today, even in this...state."

"Right...Look Sana, I can't let you swim in this condition." She argued.

"You'll have to!" I raised my voice, and plead.

"Give me one reason Sana as to why I should let you swim when you seem completely high, and out of your mind."

"Well, I'd give you three. First, I have waited for this day, ever since I joined this school. Second, soooo many people are counting on me, for this thing. Next, I really need to prove my worth to students from my last school. And lastly, I really want something good to happen with me today. Even if it's a...swimming miracle."

"Those are four reasons." She replied bluntly, without considering my answer.

But that day, I just didn't care.

I am going to swim, no matter what.

As I stepped onto the block, I felt rather calm, I could no longer feel the adrenaline rush through my body, as I had dreamt of or what I had imagined ever since I had seen Aman step onto his block thinking that someday, I'll be a swimmer who's better than him. Instead, I felt rather relaxed and tranquil. I looked to my right and saw five other swimmers, doing stretches and talking to their coaches. But all I did was stand still, and stare at the water that lay ahead of me.

It felt like the water was beckoning me to ride along with it. I suddenly got carried away by a flashback, I remembered the first time I was giving my swimming trials. I visualized standing by the edge of the pool, my legs were shivering, my hands were trembling, I had poor stamina, and was sure that I'd barely make it to the end.

But as I stood there on my block, waiting for my heat to begin, I somehow felt confident, and thought maybe it was just the cigs doing their job, making me feel calm, or whatever it was, I had a good feeling about this.

"On your mark!" Screamed the starter.

I inhaled deeply, closed my eyes as I took my position, and told myself. *I can do this.* I was meant for this.

The loud horn blew again.

As I dived into the pool, I felt my head placed in between my arms, which I thought were rotating like the wheel of a supersonic car. My legs were doing their best too, flapping up and down, breaking the layers of the water, giving the water a white, pearl color on its edges. Once again, my arms and legs were working in harmony.

But it was my mind and my lungs which weren't. Once again, I was facing difficulty in breathing, but this time I knew, all I had to do was take long breaths instead of short, whilst maintaining my speed.

It was when I had crossed the 40-meter benchmark when my body started to give in to all the torture that it had been going through not only in the last month, but moreover, the last few hours. It felt like just how all this while my minded craved the smoke this time my lungs craved for some more air.

To speed myself up, I decided to take one long breath, and pull along with that as long as possible in order to minimize time wasted on breathing. And that is when my body finally gave up on me.

I couldn't breathe. I felt that the passage to my lungs was blocked, or rather filled with water. So as a human reaction, I opened my mouth to breathe but instead of air, I consumed more water, and I didn't know how to provide myself with oxygen to breathe. I tried to make an O with my mouth, trying to inhale as much as possible, but instead, *it only made the situation worse.*

All of a sudden, my legs and arms gave up and stopped functioning the way they were supposed to do. Instead, my arms were flapping vertically, trying to stay afloat, while my legs were working in a cyclic motion, to make sure I didn't drown. However, without air being provided to them in the quantity that it should, they too couldn't help me for long.

"Help—me!" I tried to shout, but it came out as a faint whisper, due to the water that was filled in my mouth.

By then, I was almost 3–4th inside the water, when I shouted again, "I'm drown–"

It felt like my entire body just *went to power off mode*. My eyes gently closed, while my nose stopped trying to perform its normal function of *breathing.* My limbs had stopped moving, and then all that my brain could think of, and my body feel, was the unbearable pain. I knew that the tiffany blue water, which was once calling me to come and ride along, was now trying to engulf me into itself, and there was nothing that I could do to stop it or help myself.

I was drowning.

EPILOGUE

**Almost a year later;
At the inauguration ceremony.**

"Smoking is a lot like love. We cannot simply stop loving someone. We cannot simply turn off the feeling, both, the desire to be loved and to love someone. We cannot simply, quit loving. And in the same way, it is not easy to simply quit smoking either. Because I believe that there is this almost unbreakable bond which one forms with their cigarettes. For they too make one feel wanted, and needed. *It is a feeling hard to describe but it is there, and not easy to let go.*

A year ago, when I chose to quit smoking, immediately after my accident at the pool, I figured it wasn't as easy as I had imagined. I'll try to keep this short, it was a twisted, bumpy, curvy road, filled with alligators and venomous animals, and I was travelling on this road, sitting on a turtle.

In simpler language, *it was tough to quit and the process was slow.*

The venomous animal in my story was Papa. When he found out about...well everything, it wasn't a sight to be seen. I still remember, lying down in the emergency

Epilogue

room, with Papa standing on my right side and Mumma on my left. His exact words were, "You are not worth being called my daughter, or a Sharma for that matter. I disown you!" He didn't talk to me for almost a month after that.

I tried many methods to help myself quit smoking, I first went completely cold turkey. But with Papa not talking to me, it made it all the more difficult, the unbearable pain from my injury and almost no support from my family, I relapsed in just about a week. I tried to do this again in the following few weeks, but it obviously didn't work out.

So, I finally ended up with a counsellor, now a very close friend of mine, who is sitting right here, in this audience." I pointed at a thirty something lady with short hair and a dark complexion. "Had it not been for Ms. Ruchi, I would probably still be smoking a pack of cigarettes each day, which is basically like taking slow poison leading to an unseen, slow-fatal death.

She was the one who taught me to use the 'list technique,' a technique which saved me and my future. This list included all the reasons why I must quit smoking. I stuck it in just about every place of the house, my washroom, my cupboard, my bed. I kept a copy in my bag, my pencil box, basically every place one can imagine, and every time I felt the urge to smoke, I looked at the list, and I was convinced not to go ahead."

I took out a sheet of paper with words scribbled in pencil, almost the size of a palm and placed it on the dais. "I really don't need this anymore, but I found one and thought I'd read it out to you all...Well, the first item on my list was about 'my groin injury.' For those of you who don't know the whole story.... after I was taken out of the water and rushed to the hospital, the first thing I recall the doctor told Mumma, when I was in a semi-conscious state was, "She cannot swim for at least five weeks."

Later I also found out that, not stretching before swimming a 100-meter race was *not a good choice*, and one that I regretted immediately after. It was also the reason for the excruciating pain in my legs and the reason for them to stop working when I was swimming. Every time I looked at this point on the list, all I could think about was the pain and how badly I wanted to go back to swimming, so, yes, it kept me away from those *filthy cigarettes*.

The next one on the list was my 'damaged lungs.' I should have seen this one coming, with me smoking about four to five cigarettes per day, at such a young age, regularly. My lungs had become weak, because they weren't fully developed in the first place, considering that I wasn't even eighteen; and I further poisoned them with all the smoke. They had obviously become weak. This was the primary reason for my lungs to have kind of collapsed after the heavy smoking I did right before swimming.

If I recall correctly, I was told by the doctor that "my weak lungs were filled with chlorinated water" which was later pumped out using a machine, which...let's say made the whole experience *extremely unpleasant* because I remember screaming and screeching with pain, such that people outside thought I was in severe labor pain.

Epilogue

Anyway...the memory of the pain too, kept me away from buying a box of cigarettes.

Now, the third item on the list was 'losing the districts.' Although this shouldn't come as a shock, but I obviously lost in both my races at the districts. So, yes... my several weeks long training, all went down the drain, plus, I couldn't swim again for over a month.

Apart from all this, there was obviously 'Papa' on my list who made sure to make me *constantly* feel guilty about smoking, about letting his name down as a swimmer and about relapsing several times. But...after a few months Ruchi told me how to convert all this guilt into positive energy which motivated me to get rid of all the mental and physical after effects of smoking, as well as never to restart.

And I cannot miss out the last but most important item on the list, which I made sure to write in bold, red letters – *Smoking almost killed me!* And believe me, every time I looked at those words, I just knew that I didn't want to go there again."

I shoved the list back into the pocket of my pencil pants, and placed my hands on the dais. "Apart from this list, I also used nicotine patches, lozenges and literally anything that would keep me away from a cigarette, and eventually...it went away. A few months later, I got used to dealing with my problems without feeling the need to smoke. I got used to actually living life like a normal teenager. Most importantly, I started *valuing* my own life.

And as I stand here, I would like to thank Ms. Parneet Singh, for accepting me here at Spring Valley School, regardless of all those hideous news reports which publicized me as a '*drowning drug-addict*' and even after the strong negative feedback from Avenues International.

Without Ruchi, I would have probably not been able to face the fact that a good all-round student was expelled from her school, which would have probably made me smoking even more. And well...when it comes to thanking, I cannot forget my lovely, new group of *real* friends." I pointed at each one of them, sitting in the front row, "Poonam, Aditi, and Saria, who supported me and had my back as I tried to quit this awful habit completely."

I could see Aditi get teary eyed, while Poonam clapped along the audience and Saria passed me a big smile.

I won't be right if I leave out my dear parents, especially Mumma, who even after everything, believed in me, and that reminds me...once I was sitting on my bed, crying, with a box of cigarettes placed in front of me.

She came in and asked what happened, and I told her how my cold turkey plan only lasted merely a few days, and that I thought she must be so embarrassed of me. But instead, she said, "I will always love you, not only because you're my child, but because you're a good child. You're a good person who's just picked up some bad habits, and habits can always be expelled like they are developed. Just give it some time beta."

I wiped a tear that was building up on the rim of my right eye and continued, "And for Papa, well, he too eventually realized that just getting mad at me won't help, and the fact that I actually wanted to quit is a big thing, and he must support me, and that is probably the reason

Epilogue

why he helped in building and growing something that started as a random idea, into a live, functioning project."

I pointed at the screen that was displaying 'Intra-School Quit Smoking Service – ISQSS' "All of this wouldn't have been possible without you Papa." From the front row in the audience, he looked at me now with pride and eyes full of tears of joy.

A smile took over my face, "I look forward and hope that this initiative acts as a sturdy platform to help and support anyone who wants to quit smoking. It would not judge you, make you feel guilty or preach to you. My team, which is headed by Ms. Ruchi, would be there for you, at each step along the path. All you need to do is take the first step."

I continued, "Only remember one thing, it takes a lot more than just a will, one needs mental, physical as well as spiritual counselling to get out of smoking, and I know it's not easy, because I've been there, but that doesn't mean you give up, *you must keep breathing.*"

While at one point I took up smoking as the easiest way to handle my life, it was the decision to quit and rigidly sticking to it which was the turning point of my life."

And if I had to sum up my entire journey, I would say that we all have our own set of problems - be it the pressure from our society, our over demanding parents or the desire for social approval, but the bottom line is, that we need to believe in ourselves, and that there is no short cut to handling these burning truths of our lives.

Printed in Great Britain
by Amazon